There w̲  had turned a corner a̲ ̲ ̲ ̲ how or why. All she knew was that the moment he'd walked into the lounge, she wanted to be near him.

The speech concluded, and the band began to play. An old ballad wafted through the room, and couples slowly migrated to the dance floor. Megan's heart fluttered. Henry would come to ask her to dance. She knew it and didn't bother acting coy. Their dance was inevitable. She sought his gaze across the room, and he was already up from his chair and moving toward her.

She let him take her hand and guide her to the dance floor. His arm slipped around her waist and guided her closer. They danced together smoothly, the music bathing them with its sweet melody. She momentarily closed her eyes and just let herself be carried away on Henry's lead.

"That was great what you said to Carolyn before."

She opened her eyes. Henry stared at her, his head angled down, his mouth very close.

Still wrapped in the music and the feel of his body next to hers, she did not speak.

"About having a change of dreams," he reminded her.

"Oh yes. I think that's most people's experience one time or another. Having a change of dreams."

"It can be tough to do."

"It's courageous, too. Sometimes it's easier to just accept that your dream didn't come true rather than find yourself a new one."

His gaze bored into her. "What would you do if I kissed you right now?"

Praise for M. Kate Quinn

"M. Kate Quinn delivers a warm and funny story woven like a favorite blanket made with love, promise, and a second chance. Readers will curl up with *THE HOPE CHEST* and settle in for a memorable read."

~ Stacey Wilk, Author

~*~

"*THE HOPE CHEST* will make you laugh and cry, a poignant tale of love and redemption. Quinn brings her memorable characters together in a heartfelt romance."

~Shari Nichols, Award-Winning Author

~*~

"A tainted past and a second chance at love and family. *THE HOPE CHEST* is a page-turner."

~K. Quick, Author

~*~

"M. Kate Quinn writes highly romantic books, infused with humor and tenderness. This book is as well-written as the first two in the series!"

~Roni Denholtz, Award-Winning Author

The Hope Chest

by

M. Kate Quinn

The Sycamore River Series, Book 3

This is a work of fiction. Names, characters, places, and incidents are either the product of the author's imagination or are used fictitiously, and any resemblance to actual persons living or dead, business establishments, events, or locales, is entirely coincidental.

The Hope Chest

COPYRIGHT © 2021 by Marykate Schweiger

All rights reserved. No part of this book may be used or reproduced in any manner whatsoever without written permission of the author or The Wild Rose Press, Inc. except in the case of brief quotations embodied in critical articles or reviews.
Contact Information: info@thewildrosepress.com

Cover Art by *The Wild Rose Press, Inc.*

The Wild Rose Press, Inc.
PO Box 708
Adams Basin, NY 14410-0708
Visit us at www.thewildrosepress.com

Publishing History
First Edition, 2021
Trade Paperback ISBN 978-1-5092-3696-1
Digital ISBN 978-1-5092-3697-8

The Sycamore River Series, Book 3
Published in the United States of America

Dedication

To my grandson, Ean Michael Hemsey
With your innate athleticism, your keen eye,
and that unquenchable thirst for learning,
the world awaits you, my darling boy.

Chapter One

Henry Denhawk winced at the sight of his face in the mirror hanging over the credenza in his living room. The swelling around his eye had gone down since the other night, but now a rainbow of colors decorated his cheekbones.

He did his best to ignore his agent's narrow-eyed glare as he looked on. Cliff's face was beet red, his hairy-knuckled hands balled into fists, and Henry knew from experience more ranting was on its way.

"Damn it, man," the wired-too-tight Cliff spat. "I still can't believe you let some punk in a bar push your buttons. Christ Almighty. What were you thinking, Hank?"

Henry groaned, and his temples began to throb. "Can you stop asking me that?"

"No. I need to understand. You're not some kid in a schoolyard. You're a grown-ass man. I mean, hello. You're pushing forty."

Henry fixed his gaze on the ceiling. "Somebody just shoot me." He strode away from the mirror, from the telltale image of his puffy face, and went into the kitchen. Cliff uttered an expletive and followed, his wingtip dress shoes clicking on the flooring as he rushed across the hardwood.

In the high-tech, almost-never-used kitchen, Cliff poked a finger in Henry's face. "I'm working my ass off trying to get you the broadcasting gig with the Mets, the color commentator spot you begged me to pull out of a magic freakin' hat—"

Henry snickered. "I don't beg."

"Yeah, sure. Keep lying to yourself. That'll really help the situation." He adjusted the wire-rimmed glasses that sat on his beak. "What kills me is that just when the top brass started listening to me sing your praises, which at the moment kind of makes me want to vomit up a perfectly wonderful lunch, you pull another one of your sophomoric stunts."

"Cliff—"

"No." He held up his hand, gold-and-diamond pinky ring glinting in the beam of light pouring in the kitchen window. "Let's recap, shall we? You went into some sleazeball club, hauled off, and tackled some shmuck running his mouth. For what? Your goddamn ego? And for good measure, somebody had the great idea to take a video of the event on their phone and then posted it all over the internet. Perfect."

Throat constricted, Henry charged to the fridge for a bottle of water. He yanked open the appliance, the door swinging on its hinges, and grabbed a bottle. After twisting the top off and tossing it onto the counter to skid into the toaster he never used, he guzzled the cool water and drained the bottle dry.

Cliff stood there with his hands on his hips, like a gunslinger. Glasses crooked on his face, he blew out an exaggeratedly loud breath that was half groan.

Drama queen.

"Because of your, shall we say, indiscretion, now it's my job to work a miracle. Happy now?"

Henry tossed the empty water bottle into the sink.

Cliff had been his agent for the four years since his career blew up and he'd sent his former lying snake of an agent packing.

Yet just when he was sure the world of baseball was lost to him, Cliff Jordan had sought him out and with his Napoleon-complex bravado had convinced Henry that maybe, just maybe, he still had a chance to sustain a career in the pro-ball industry even if his pitching days were over. At that time, he'd had no plans beyond getting himself healed and out of the hospital. But Cliff had been persistent, a royal pain who would not take no for an answer.

The middle-aged curmudgeon had come on board after Henry had fired his piece-of-crap agent, Michael Braddock, the lying, two-timing son of a bitch who was sleeping with Stephanie right behind his stupid back.

Cliff might be a dramatic pain in the ass, but Henry trusted him. That was saying a lot because basically, these days he trusted nobody.

He met his agent's dark stare. "I'm sorry I let you down. Okay? If I could undo it, Cliff, I would."

He'd never been the kind of guy to swing his fists, had spent his twelve years of pro baseball doing his job with all he had and loving it. Yeah, he'd partied too much and enjoyed carousing around with his buddies. But he'd taken his job as the Mets' starting pitcher seriously.

Until four years ago when he'd had too many hot toddies in Aspen and decided skiing down the double black diamond slope was a good idea after finding his girl and Michael in bed. Turned out the snake had been sleeping with Stephanie for months. To top it off, the two were man and wife now.

That reckless trip down the mountain had cost Henry everything. A decimated shoulder and a crushed elbow and his pitching career had gone to shit.

He willed his brain to block out the memories of how he'd struggled through the last four years. At thirty-five and with such severe injuries, he'd given the franchise the perfect excuse to cut him loose. Cliff had negotiated a partial buyout, but now four years later, he was spitting in the wind. He needed the broadcasting job, wanted it like air, and he knew he'd be an asset to the Mets' commentator roster. But another stupid night and too much whiskey found him jabbing his fist at some jerk's big mouth. Now the media was all over it and dredging up his asinine behavior of four years ago.

As much as he hated to agree with Cliff's current frenzy, he really was in a self-induced mess, and in all likelihood, he'd screwed his chance in broadcasting. He didn't ever freakin' learn.

He opened a cabinet and searched for something to munch on, something to release his jaw's clench. He withdrew a plastic container of almonds and quickly scooped a handful into his palm. If he had his mouth full, he didn't have to talk to Cliff, who was still scowling.

"Since when do you listen to assholes slinging insults?" Cliff climbed onto a backless stool and opened his laptop on the granite island. "Some drunk calls you a loser, and what do you do? You act like one."

"How is this helping?"

"I'll tell you how." Cliff shifted in his seat, adjusted his glasses. "This little stunt confirms what I've thought all along. You need a change. And that's why you're going back to your little hometown,

Suwanee River."

"Sycamore River, smart-ass. And no, thanks."

"You're going, and you'll graciously accept the invitation to speak at your high school baseball coach's retirement celebration. And you're going to RSVP yes to that invite you got for the shindig the town is throwing for its anniversary. No ifs, ands, or buts."

"I don't even remember when either one of those things is. I must have deleted the email for the coach's thing and thrown away the anniversary invitation. Oops."

"Fear not, wise guy. Lucky for you I copied the information to my calendar. The coach's retirement ceremony is on Friday at three p.m. I've just RSVP'd that you'll be there. With. Bells. On. The gala is on Saturday, October fifteenth. You responded that you'd be delighted to attend."

Henry grimaced, and his face hurt, but he suppressed a wince. Why give Cliff more ammo? "And you think my appearing at those events is going to cool the jets of all the media hounds out there? Come on, Cliff, my mug's all over the internet right now."

"I'm painfully aware. These hometown appearances of the great Henry Denhawk will be the beginning of our changing your image."

"What are you talking about?"

Cliff closed his laptop with a flourish. "As of today, life as you knew it is bye-bye. New York City has done you no favors. Hanging out at all those local watering holes getting into trouble, playing darts like a frat boy, roughhousing. No more bachelor gone wild."

He couldn't help it. He laughed. "Bachelor gone wild?"

"You heard me. And no more of all those skinny girls you date with their unmoving fake contours. You know, those underfed model types that look like tits on a stick. Done."

"Like hell I am." He shot up from the stool he'd straddled and sent it tipping over behind him. He made a face and sucked in his breath at the pain it caused, then let out a string of curses—heavy-duty ones, the kind saved for locker rooms and poker games with the boys.

"Nice. Hope you enjoyed that." Cliff shook his head. "As of now, no more potty mouth either. You want to be a spokesperson for a major league franchise? Act like a gentleman."

"You first."

"Very funny. Maybe if this doesn't work out, you can do stand-up. Seriously, Hank. We need to get you away from this reputation you've created for yourself. Roger Dennis, remember him? The head guy in broadcasting? He said you'd be a shoo-in if it weren't for the negative buzz going on about you. It's dredging up what happened four years ago. Congratulations, you relit that fire with a blowtorch."

"Please stop."

"It's my job—correct that, our job—to clean up how the world at large sees you. No more rag mags with your photo plastered on the front with some bimbo who a month later accuses you of reneging on a marriage proposal, or claims a fake pregnancy."

"Cliff, listen to me. Those women can be in my rearview mirror, okay? But I live here in New York. I like it here. I actually have obligations with the carpenters I've been working with. We're in the middle of redoing a screened-in porch. I can't just walk away from that. And in case you were thinking I can just up and walk away, there are five or six months left on my lease, so I'm not uprooting. That's insane. What do you expect me to do? Become a hermit? A celibate monk?"

"That I'd like to see, but no. First off, screw the carpentry. Call them up and tell them you're otherwise engaged. You've got bigger fish to fry. You're going to immerse yourself in community service, something wholesome that'll make a nice story in print. We're going to make sure all the news outlets become fully aware of your philanthropic gestures. We're going to resurrect the guy you used to be before you decided to be a horse's ass."

Henry groaned. "I'm not buying into any of this, and neither will anyone reading nice-guy stories about me in the tabloids."

"Well, we're going to do it, Hank. It's our best shot. We need to make you lovable again."

"Oh, for God's sake."

Cliff plastered on a broad grin. "This is going to be fun. For me, anyway."

Henry raked fingers through his hair. "I need a drink."

"That's another thing. You're off the sauce for now."

"Says who?"

"Says me. You can have a glass of wine with dinner like civilized people. That's it."

"You're insane."

"Tell me that when you're doing the commentating for the upcoming major league season."

Henry paced back and forth in front of his kitchen

island. He wouldn't admit it to Cliff, but he was well aware that blame for this crapola was on him and him alone. Somehow, he'd let an asshole in a bar push his hot button with just one simple little word. It rang in his ears now, taunting him. *Loser.*

He was not a loser, but whenever the word surfaced, a reel of his stunt from four years ago played in his head. Getting just drunk enough to lose his perspective had given him license to act like a fool. Finding out his girlfriend was messing around behind his back with his agent at the Aspen lodge was a double betrayal that sent him over the edge. He'd been such an idiot to believe in love and crazy enough to pluck the diamond ring he'd been prepared to give her from its velvet box and flush the damn thing down the toilet. Like a movie playing out in his head, the images wouldn't stop, the *on* switch having been flipped by the trigger of that one little word.

"You with me, Hank? You look like you've seen a ghost."

He focused his gaze on Cliff, whose scowl caused folds of frustration to crease his forehead like one of those wrinkly dogs, a shar-pei. A venomous urge tempted him to voice his observation, but he held his tongue. This wet blanket was quite possibly the only guy on the planet that could make him a broadcaster for his beloved Mets. And he wanted it. Really wanted it. Before the accident, he'd have been able to write his own ticket anywhere. He'd been the man, the player all the fans chanted to when he stepped out onto the field.

But this was now.

"You know, Cliff, I can't believe the hoops I have to jump through now. Sometimes it's hard to believe that I'm still Henry Denhawk." His nickname had sounded in a tsunami-like wave through the stands whenever he was on the mound, and the memory rose in his mind now. "Did I really used to be that guy? Was I really the Hawk?"

Cliff studied him, his eyes quizzical, as though he were trying to decide if the big lug standing in front of him were indeed the former baseball star, the famous *Hawk*. His face softened, and one corner of his mouth turned into a rueful half grin. "Come on, Hank. Let's make this work."

Henry never thought he'd step foot back in his hometown. Sycamore River held nothing for him now. His mom, his only relative, was gone, and there was no one else he wanted or needed to see.

But that was just where he was headed on Friday. He thought of his mother, who had died a little more than five years ago. She'd been the one person who believed in him no matter what. She hadn't lived to see the debacle of four years ago, but history told him she'd have still been there for him. What had he done to deserve it?

"On Friday," he said, not looking directly at Cliff, "I want to go into Sycamore River a bit early. I'd like to stop off at the cemetery and pay respects to my mother."

"Great idea. I'll take pictures and leak them to the media."

"For God's sake, Cliff. Stop."

"Desperate times, desperate measures, my friend."

Chapter Two

Megan Harris ran her hand over the newly restored hope chest, the rich mahogany gleaming in the sunlight coming in the store's large bay window. She cast her gaze to the alcove area up front by the cash register where the prized cabinet would be displayed, the perfect spot for the beautiful piece to entice shoppers.

Still so much to do before her thrift shop would be ready for business. Halloween was the target date of its official opening, which left her with just weeks to get everything done. Where had this week gone? It was Friday already.

"I better not break a nail." Lucy, Megan's best friend, stood at the other end of the chest. The petite blonde wore her typical businessy outfit, pencil skirt and a smart blazer, two-inch heels. "I'm showing a house to clients in less than a half hour, so let's get this manual labor over with. Chop, chop. Just a thought, though. Why can't we simply go out back and get one of those hunks to come in here and move this sucker?"

The hunks Lucy referred to were the crew of workers hired by Megan's landlord, Sid, to restore the building's back steps. Although Lucy enjoyed the "eye candy," as she called it, Megan regarded the presence of the workmen as more of a nuisance. As long as the back entrance to the building was inaccessible, the only way for Sid to get to his upstairs apartment was through

Megan's storefront. And Sid liked to chat. She had no time for it.

"We're not interrupting those guys out there. The sooner they're done and out of here, the better."

"Seriously?" Lucy placed her hands on her hips. "That's all you've got to say about those specimens?"

"Hey, until the steps are done, I'm at the mercy of Sid's need to *shoot the breeze*."

"But you like the old guy, right?"

"Yes, of course. Sid's great. But I'm on a deadline, and I've got work to do. This store's not going to open on its own."

A pang of guilt tickled her at midchest. Sidney Goldman was a sweet old guy, a gem of a landlord, and he was lonely. She could spot lonely at ten paces. Twenty.

Each day he'd come into her store after one of his jaunts into town, dressed in a suit and tie as if he were ready for a party, and strike up a conversation. Many times, he'd convinced Megan to join him for "cocktail hour" up in his apartment, where he'd have cheese and crackers arranged on a dinner plate, and he'd pour her a glass of chardonnay he purchased just for her. She shook the thoughts of Sidney from her head.

"I just need to get this done."

Lucy nodded. "I understand. I do. But, honey, all work and no play…"

Megan blew out a long breath. "Lucy, I played when I went to Kit's bachelorette party. Remember? I made a monumental ass out of myself. So I'm sticking to work. I'm better at it."

If only Lucy knew the sordid details of that night she'd spent in New York City, where a gaggle of Kit

Baxter's friends had gathered to celebrate her upcoming wedding to her fireman fiancé, Shamus.

Megan hadn't wanted to go to the bachelorette party and was prepared to beg off, but Lucy wouldn't have it. She picked out an outfit for Megan and applied her makeup with a more daring hand than Megan ever used. She expertly fluffed Megan's chestnut hair into an alluring mane. When Megan complained that the long side bangs were in her eyes and annoying the hell out of her, Lucy swatted at her hand.

"Stop. You look sexy like that. Go and just let loose for once," Lucy said.

The party happened to fall just after the second anniversary of William's death. Maybe the date was the catalyst for her behavior that night. She had been a widow for what felt like so long she forgot what it was like to go to a club with friends, have some drinks, and laugh it up. At thirty-eight she mostly felt like an old lady, and her best friend wasn't having it. So wearing one of Lucy's skimpy can't-wear-a-bra silk tops, in the color she coined as "ho red," and skintight black crop pants, she reluctantly promised Lucy before she left that she'd let herself have fun.

Lucy did not know how her protégé had excelled at that promise. She'd known about Megan's hookup, but she didn't know the half of it. Keeping the sordid details from Lucy was a daily feat.

Since the party was held around the time of the tragic anniversary, Megan's promise to Lucy hadn't been mere lip service. She'd meant it when she agreed to have a good time for once in a long, long while. Only who could have foreseen that two whopping margaritas with top-shelf tequila and an oozingly hot guy at the bar would have flooded her mind and body with feeling, drowning her with want so intense she shook? Her loneliness for a man's touch, her being so very weary from widowhood, and the fervent need to feel alive, even for just one night, had propelled her to take the reins in that seduction. For a moment she'd been kind of proud of her daring, only to feel lower than she'd ever felt in her life when it was over. And more alone.

"As your dearest friend, I have to tell you that you're going backward. You need to go out and have fun on a more regular basis, not just once in a blue moon. Take a break, Megs. You'll still get all your work done. Ease up a little."

"I'll take that under advisement, okay? Now let's carry this cabinet over to its display area so you can go sell a house to your clients and I can go stop by the cemetery."

"Megs…"

Lucy was going to tell her she was overdoing it by visiting the cemetery every Friday to bring a rose to William's headstone, but ever since the night of the hookup, the sourness of betrayal sat in her belly as if she'd cheated on her husband. She needed to visit William if only to remember who she'd been when he was alive.

"It's drizzling out and foggy as hell. Are you sure you can't skip it just this once? Come on, Megan. Ease up on that, too."

"Can't. I have to go, and when I get back here, I'm meeting up with Sid to give him my rent check." A wry smile came to her lips. "And, of course, he roped me into joining him for a drink. I felt too bad to turn him down."

"You're a good egg, Megan. I'm glad you're going to spend some time with the old guy, but you need your own kind of distraction, some tall, dark, and handsome tension breaker."

"Please. I've had my share of handsome strangers. Let's just move this hope chest." She positioned herself at one end of the cabinet. "Come on."

Lucy placed her hands on the other end of the chest. "I'm not talking about another hookup. It's obvious that's not your comfort zone. But how about enjoying the company of a man again? Start out with something small, like going for coffee or a drink."

Megan groaned. Her friend was determined to get her back into the world of dating, and she just wasn't ready. William had been gone for two years, but some days she still bore the heaviness of loss, and sometimes the reality of widowhood parked itself in her chest like a brick. The hookup had only intensified her feelings.

"Meg, you just need someone to flirt with a little, have some fun with. Someone like, say, Peter Moss, for example, the guy who owns the bookstore. He's widowed too and kind of, um, interesting looking in his own way."

Megan narrowed her gaze. "You do realize the guy's name is Pete Moss."

"What's in a name? Maybe he's *earthy*."

"Um, no."

Lucy chuckled. "Okay, too much like mulch." She wiggled her expertly arched eyebrows. "How about one of those hunks of manhood working outside?" She pointed a finger toward the doorway at the back of the store. "Flirt with one of them, and while you're at it, have him come in here and move this hunk of wood for us."

Flirt a little? That was what she'd intended the night of the bachelorette party. No. A thousand times no.

She owed something to William's memory. He'd been the man who strolled into the retro-looking diner she'd worked at in Chicago. He'd wooed her over time, lavished her with unfamiliar attention, and eventually proposed. William had whisked her away from her cold and drafty efficiency apartment over the drugstore to live in a nice house in this nice town in New Jersey. If it hadn't been for him, she'd probably still be slinging hash. He'd given her a life, a suburban life in a storybook house with eight rooms and a cleaning lady who came every other Thursday. She shared a perfect life with William, and Megan could never figure out why she'd felt such unrest in it. She was ashamed to admit to herself that most of the time she'd felt as if someone had dropped her in Oz.

After William died, their eight-room colonial hadn't felt like home anymore. She'd rattled around the echoing rooms day after day until she couldn't take it anymore. Thanks to Lucy's expertise in real estate, they'd listed the house, and it sold within a couple of weeks. She'd used much of the proceeds to start up her thrift shop.

Thrift shops had saved her existence when she lived alone in Chicago. Now she had the chance to help others. And that would have to be her fulfillment.

She ignored her friend's urging and reached over to take hold of the old brass key that protruded from the hope chest's lock. She locked the cabinet, securing the lid tight, and slipped the key into the pocket of her long, oversize cardigan.

"Ready?"

"Do you ever just relax?"

Megan shook her head. "Overrated. Now on three, we lift."

Chapter Three

Henry drove his truck in through the large wrought-iron gates of the cemetery in Sycamore River and parked at the curbing along the headstones marked at row thirty-four. How long had it been since he came to pay respects to his mother? *Respects.* The word made him cringe. He was a little short on respect these days.

The large tan dog in the back seat of his overpriced, overly large SUV woke from a noisy snoring slumber. The pooch bolted upright, doing God only knew what to his imported leather seat. The dog uttered a loud woof.

Henry's agent turned in his seat on the passenger side and reprimanded the dog. "Settle down, Frito."

The dog only barked some more. Cliff pinched a thumb and forefinger to the bridge of his nose.

"Did you have to bring that mutt with you?"

"I wish I hadn't. Why my wife loves this animal is beyond me. If she doesn't come home from her sister's soon, I might ship him to her UPS."

The dog attempted to wedge himself between the front seats, getting his upper torso stuck. He let out an ear-piercing yelp.

"For crying out loud, Cliff. What's with this mutt? Aren't dogs supposed to be smart? How'd he get himself stuck like that? And that whining's piercing my eardrums. Maybe he needs a muzzle."

"That's big coming from a grown-ass man sporting a shiner from a bar fight. Maybe you're the one who needs a muzzle." Cliff gave Frito a shove that freed him. He patted the animal's head. "Don't listen to Henry. He's a grouch. And he doesn't learn by his mistakes either."

Henry groaned. "Will you stop?"

"Are you ready for this event this afternoon?"

"As I'll ever be." He wanted to go back to his old high school, see all the old teachers who were still there, and speak for Coach Brennen like he wanted his fingernails ripped out of their beds. But he had no choice. This personal appearance could be putting him one step closer to getting the gig with major league baseball. Who wouldn't want to be a color commentator for the New York Mets? If he couldn't play the game anymore, this opportunity was the best he could hope for. And he'd get it, too. He had to.

Henry unclipped his seat belt and turned to face his agent. "Now can I go have a moment alone while I pay a visit to my mother's grave?"

"Make sure you stand sideways so when I take your picture, people will know it's you."

"No picture."

"What are you talking about?" Cliff snorted. "This will make good promo for you."

Henry groaned. "You're giving me a headache."

"Yeah, well, blame yourself."

The fur ball in the back seat hopped up and down as if to agree with his master. Henry swung open the driver's side door. "Don't follow me. Don't take my picture. And keep that damn dog quiet."

The fog was thick and billowy, the perfect scene

for a cemetery if he were in a monster movie. His good shoes squished in the wet ground. He pulled up the collar of his jacket to ward against the fine mist spraying his face and head.

He made his way across the lawn toward his mother's gravesite. A gust of chilly October air rushed at him, and he pulled his jacket closer.

An oversize, fat, purple mum had been planted at his mother's headstone. Purple had been Mom's favorite color. Only one person could have planted the flowers, and his instant jab of disdain shamed even him. He hadn't seen his stepfather in the four years since he left town, and considering they hated each other with a passion, he'd make sure to steer clear of the guy while he was in town.

He focused his gaze on the letters expertly etched into the granite. His mother's name gave him a pang. Olivia Maria Goldman. She'd been the one person he could count on, the one person who'd have been in his corner even after he sabotaged his career. Having passed six months prior to his debacle, Mom hadn't known how he wrecked his pitching arm and tanked his career. That was one good thing.

He closed his eyes and tried to inwardly say something to her, conjure a makeshift prayer maybe, but words would not come. Talking to a cube of granite felt weird. This wasn't his mother. Gone was gone.

****

Megan was pretty sure that cursing in a cemetery was taboo, but she did it anyway. She'd forgotten about the rain and the wet lawn. Her designer flats, shoes she'd owned for years and kept pristine, sank into the goopy earth as she crossed the aisle toward William's grave. The shoes would be ruined, and she was not in the position to replace them. These days her footwear came from what she could find on a department store's sale rack.

With the one long-stemmed red rose in her hand, she trod with the caution of a soldier sidestepping landmines to avoid any chance of a rogue splash of mud that could soil her hand-knit coat sweater. She should have dressed for combat, for crying out loud.

She stood at William's grave as she had every Friday. *Two years.* How was it possible that her husband had been gone for that long when some days the sorrow gripped her as if it were new?

"Oh, William. I still can't believe it. Two years is a long time." She touched the top of his headstone, the cold droplets of rainwater chilling her fingertips. "I passed our house the other day while I was on my way to an estate sale. It looks nice, cared for. I know how much you liked that house. I never really felt at home there. But you knew that. Remember when I wanted to paint the front door yellow and you vetoed it? You'd said a yellow door was too folksy for such a big grand house. Maybe that was my problem. I was too folksy for that house."

Suddenly her skin prickled with the feeling of being watched. She looked down the long row of stones and saw a tall, blondish man in a khaki jacket staring at her. He was handsome with that upturned collar and his shock of wheat-colored hair tousled from the breeze. A stab of reprimand pierced her chest. She had to stop noticing levels of handsomeness in random men. She'd let it get her into an outlandish situation once, and once was enough.

"Turn sideways," another man called out from a black truck parked along the curbing. He had his door open and stood on the running board while aiming his cell phone at the handsome guy by the gravestone.

"No," he called back, his voice gruff. "Stop it."

The man's phone sounded, and suddenly a big tan dog jumped out from the truck's open door and bolted across the grass at full speed, barking like crazy.

"Frito," the man in the truck yelled. "Jesus, Hank, catch that dog."

"Oh, for God's sake. It's your dog. You get him."

"I'm on the phone. Hank, get him!"

The dog was headed right for her, and she instinctively took a step backward as she sucked in her breath. The muddy beast pounced on her, tongue flapping in the breeze, and she tried to wrestle free. His forepaws pressed onto her sweater, and she shouted at him. "Get down."

His mighty jaw grabbed the perfect bloom from her hand, and he charged away, spraying goopy mud in his wake.

"My rose!"

The blond guy tried to corner the dog, but the animal darted away. "Damn it, Frito, drop that flower." The dog ran faster, circled around, and did a little hop that said, "Let's play."

Megan ran in the direction of the dog, following the guy. She liked dogs—most of them, anyway—and tried to coax this one to come to her.

"Here, boy," she cooed. "Come on. Come here, good boy."

The dog paused by the first headstone and locked his black eyes on to her, his head cocked as if he were trying to decide if she was telling the truth. The blond guy approached, and the dog took off in his game of chase. He followed the dog, who ran left, then right and round and round the headstones. Megan closed in on them and reached for the dog, tripping on the damp grass. She fell to her knees, palms and knees muddied. She swore and didn't care.

"Shit, are you all right?" the man asked. He tried to reach the dog, who was too fast for him.

She stood up and groaned at the muddy dirt marks on the knees of her jeans. "Just get my damned rose."

Finally, he grabbed the dog by its collar and yanked the stem from his jaw. The petals had all but fallen off the bloom, and the long stem was gnarled and bent in half. The dog freed himself from the guy's grasp and ran back to the other man at the truck, who had started to shake a bag of dog treats.

Sheepishly, the guy handed her the misshapen, mutilated rose. She took it and uttered a sound of disgust. The collar of the man's jacket fell away from his face as he lifted a hand and raked long fingers through his damp hair. Then it hit her like a bulldozer on full throttle.

In utter disbelief and heart stalled in her chest, she took in the guy's countenance, the chiseled planes of his face, dewy and damp from the mist in the air, the full mouth, the perfect brows, and the crystalline blue eyes. *Holy shit. Shit, shit, shit*. This had to be some kind of cosmic joke. It was him. The hookup guy from Kit's bachelorette party. Standing here in the cemetery of all places.

"You." The word shot from her mouth.

Confusion shone in his eyes for a beat, an

insultingly long beat, then like a cloud moving across the sky, recognition came into his stunning eyes. "Well, what do you know?" That sexy, I'm-pure-trouble half smile curved one side of his come-kiss-me mouth.

She swore again in the cemetery, certain she would go to hell.

This tall, handsome bad decision of hers was supposed to be gone and should have stayed gone. Annoyance ratcheted higher.

"What is wrong with you?" Her hands clenched into fists as her heart drummed in her chest. "A cemetery is supposed to be a place of peace and tranquility. And you're here disturbing everybody." She looked around. Besides his cohort in the truck, they were the only two people in sight. "The dead," she qualified. "You're disturbing the dead."

"Hey, I'm sorry about this, okay?"

He did not sound one bit contrite in her estimation. How drunk had she been that night of the bachelorette party to not notice this guy was a superficial clod?

"No." She sounded belligerent to her own ears but decided so what. For good measure, she folded her arms over her chest. "It's not okay, frankly. That beast should be on a leash. He's dangerous."

He laughed. "Dangerous? Seriously? A big goofball, maybe, but the dog's not dangerous."

"Your being here with an untethered animal is negligent. It's probably against the law. I should report you."

His jaw set then, his mouth forming a straight line. "Maybe the poor mutt was just curious to see who you were talking to. Maybe he wanted to join the party."

Megan snickered. As long as she lived, she'd never

drink another margarita. Tequila was not her friend. What had she seen in this guy? Hadn't she noticed that beyond his deliciousness he was obviously a colossal ass? "Were you actually listening to my private conversation?"

"It's kind of hard not to notice somebody talking to the dead like they were at a meet and greet."

She charged away from him. "Go to hell."

"Wait. You want us to pay to get your clothes laundered?"

She didn't respond. She just wanted to get the hell away from him.

She tossed the ruined rose into a metal garbage can and yanked open her driver's side door.

Driving away, she stole a glance into her rearview mirror. The hookup guy and the other man were in what appeared to be a heated exchange, perhaps each blaming the other for the rogue pooch.

Big fat jerks. How lousy was it that this oaf had been the guy to touch her in such a sexy way, made her feel like a woman again, kissed her until her heart felt like it might burst through her chest, nuzzled her neck, kissed the shamrock tattoo on her left inner wrist? He'd smiled a dazzling smile when he lifted his head from the tattoo kiss and said, "An Irish lass," as though such a moniker was one of royalty. Dear Jose Cuervo, where did he come from? Hadn't he told her that he lived in the city? What the hell was he doing in Sycamore River?

Chapter Four

Back at her shop Megan made her way directly to the storage room where she'd set up a kind of respite for herself. The sofa from her old house, TV, laptop, kitchenette, and bathroom served as her home away from home since she was currently staying with Lucy at her place. Lucy had found a buyer for Megan's big house so quickly she hadn't had time to find a place of her own. She wasn't complaining, considering that sale had given her the funds to start up her thrift shop. She would eventually buy a home, a small cottage hopefully, but first things first.

She peeled off her jeans, cursing the dog and the damned hookup guy who hadn't been able to stop the pooch from tackling her. She pretreated the knees of her jeans with a squirt of dish soap and shoved them into a tote to bring home for washing.

Her new sweater was dirty and would have to be hand-washed. She filled the bathroom sink with cool water and a dab of soap and plunged the sweater into the suds.

She changed into her work clothes, pulling on her denim overalls and a long-sleeved striped tee, an outfit that would have caused William to furrow his brow. She could not explain the errant sense of satisfaction that thought gave her. She wasn't mad at her poor deceased husband. But she was beyond pissed at the hookup guy who had the audacity to pause when he first saw her. He'd really paused. It sucked to high heaven that he'd stared at her for an insultingly long moment, his ridiculously handsome face advertising his bewilderment at trying to conjure where he might have seen her before. Which meant, her mind taunted, that he also did not remember, however briefly, that his goddamn mouth had been here, there, and everywhere on her skin. Mortification came to her like ice cream's brain freeze, only minus the fun part of enjoying a cone.

She went to the front desk and pulled out her checkbook and a pen. She hated writing this monthly check, and with each stroke of ink, she cursed it. Giving Aunt Gemma a check for two hundred and fifty dollars each and every month ever since she'd met William wouldn't hurt so much if it simply meant that she was helping the woman who'd taken her in after her mother died. But this was hush money she mailed to Chicago each month, and the idea that her only living relative would demand money to keep her mouth shut just pissed her off. She was pissed off at herself more than she even was of her shyster aunt, who'd never treated her like family but like a burden. She'd been nothing more than a meal ticket, considering the government paid the woman to keep Megan under her roof.

She slipped the check into an envelope and addressed it. It would go out in the morning mail. Next, she wrote out her monthly rent check to Sid Goldman, the effort more akin to a feeling of accomplishment. This payment represented her establishment of a store she called her own.

Trying her best to dismiss the sourness of her mood, she headed to tackle the cartons of glassware from the estate sale. Work would calm her down. She still couldn't believe her one-night stand was here in town and she'd come face-to-face with him in the cemetery of all places. Just when she'd hoped she'd be able to erase that night from her memory. Now it was fresh in her mind, mixed, of course, with the stupidity she felt for having chosen such an ass of a guy to be her one and only hookup.

She checked her watch. She had an hour before she was due to meet up with Sid in his upstairs apartment. Regret for agreeing to join him gave her a quick stab, but she couldn't disappoint the old guy at this short notice. Besides, spending time with him would be a nice distraction from her miserable day.

Eager to dig into a task, any task, she opened the flaps of the cardboard carton and withdrew one of the items. After shedding its paper wrapping, she examined the cut-glass gravy boat in her hands.

She turned it over and inspected the piece from all sides. It was perfect. Her nerves settled down as she held the delicate piece. Who had owned this? How many times had the pretty vessel sat on someone's holiday table? Had the gravy it held been from a family recipe handed down through the ages?

How would she put a price on a treasure that belonged to yesterday? She ran her fingers over the precision of the facets. Suddenly her mind played an image of when she'd packed up William's clothes for Goodwill—the trim-cut dress shirts with french cuffs and the pure wool slacks and blazers. It had been a sad day, a time of finality in her mind as she stared at the empty drawers of his bureau. But hopefully, his clothes had been put to someone's good use.

She tilted her head to inspect the item again, deciding she would price the gravy boat affordable enough that someone would come into her store and not be able to pass it by. Someone who would fall in love with the item, take it home, and give the vintage gravy boat a new life. Her heart did a little zip. Not even open yet, the Hope Chest would soon breathe life into old and forgotten treasures. But maybe her thrift shop would do more than save old cabinets and gravy boats. With any luck it would restore her to a life that meant something, something more than barrenness, more than the shame of a past mistake and a recent one with a guy in a bar. She hoped.

Her attention went back to the hope chest that looked perfect in its display spot in the front of the store. She walked over to the cabinet, wanting to feel the smooth wood on her fingertips. The history of the chest haunted her and sent a slew of questions to her mind. Who would give up such a lovely chest? Had its original owner found the love she hoped for? Had it been passed down to another woman in her family, a daughter perhaps or a sister? What treasures had been stashed in the chest over the years? She'd never know.

This piece of furniture was a beauty, but it was not for sale. Her shop's namesake would be the focal point of the store, viewable from the big front window, and hopefully incentive for passersby to come in and browse.

Brushing her fingers over the surface again, she eyed the keyhole. *The key!* What had she done with it? She thought back to when she and Lucy moved the chest and remembered that she'd slipped the brass key into the pocket of her new cardigan, the sweater that was soaking in a sink full of soapy water.

She dashed to the back room and quickly drained the water from the sink. Her hands gently squeezed the water from the sweater and transferred the soggy garment onto a towel. She frantically ran her hands around in the mounds of suds in the sink, fished her finger into the drain. No key.

Although she was positive she'd put the item into her sweater pocket, she checked the pockets of her dirtied jeans just to make sure. She checked her purse, knowing the effort was futile. Somehow between her visit to the cemetery and her washing the sweater, she had lost the hope chest's old brass key. Damn it to hell! The cabinet couldn't stay locked forever. What kind of omen was it that a locker of hopes was inaccessible? Would a locksmith be able to produce another key? She stifled a groan, thinking of her game of chase at the cemetery. The key could be anywhere. She swore like a sailor, glad no one was around to disapprove.

Four o'clock arrived in no time. Instead of cocktails with her landlord, what she really wanted to do was retrace today's steps, check her car's interior, walk the grassy knoll of the cemetery to see if she could locate the hope chest's key. But it would be dark soon, and the chances of finding the small item would be slim. She would have to wait and go in search tomorrow morning.

She made her way to the back staircase. The masons—the hunks, as Lucy called them—were gone for the day. She peeked out the back-door window to check on the progress of the new steps, not that she knew whether cemented cinderblocks stacked on top of each other meant they were any closer to finishing.

She'd be sure to ask Sid if he knew anything about the project's state of completeness.

She climbed the stairs to the old guy's apartment and rapped her knuckles on the dark wooden door. The soft, balladic sounds of forties music drifted from inside. In the four months she'd been Sid's tenant, she'd learned of his fascination with the musical greats of the post-World War II era. Sinatra was his favorite, but today the voice was female. She surprised herself by recognizing the lyrics, Doris Day singing about what will be will be. *Ain't that the truth?* She knocked on Sid's door again. Still he did not answer.

She called out his name. No response. A niggle of concern climbed up her spine, although she could think of no logical reason for the feeling. Although Sidney Goldman was well into his seventies, he seemed healthy and spry despite the cane he brought with him that she sometimes thought was a prop rather than a walking aid. Why was he not answering his door? Had he fallen asleep? Should she just leave him be? Something told her no.

She tried again. "Sid. It's me, Megan." *Knock. Knock.*

"Sid?" She swallowed hard and grabbed the brass doorknob. It twisted easily, and the door opened.

Stepping into the vestibule of his large apartment, she craned her neck to peek into the dining room. The Duncan Phyfe table sat empty, the cherry wood gleaming in the fading sunlight coming in through the blinds. Mookie, Sid's orange tabby cat, hopped toward her with a loud meow. She bent to give the animal a head-to-tail swoop of her hand.

"How are you today, Mookie?" He mewed again.

"Where's Sid, huh, kitty?"

She made her way through the dining room and peered into the kitchen.

Sid lay face down on the floor, shattered glass peppering the tiles next to him. The bottle of chardonnay he'd proudly told her he purchased just for her was tipped over the counter, and the pale liquid had splashed into a puddle on the floor.

She darted to him and crouched by his head. His eyes were closed as if he were sleeping, and a pointy stab of memory cut into her thoughts. When she'd gone to William in his hospital room after the kind-eyed doctor informed her he'd passed, her husband had appeared to be sleeping, too, the white blanket tucked neatly up to his chest, but he hadn't been. He'd succumbed to the injuries of his accident. Gone.

She tentatively touched Sid's bony shoulder and gave it a gentle shove. "Sid?" She swallowed. "Wake up, Sid." He did not move. The vine of panic snaking up her spine cinched its hold. Her voice was thick. "Please wake up, Sid." She eyed the way his legs were unnaturally askew and bit down on her lip. This was bad.

She needed to act and force away the feeling of floating above the scene. She breathed in and out. Who could she call? As far as she knew, Sidney had no family, no one close. Her shaking hand fumbled for the phone in her pocket, and she stabbed the keys for 911.

Chapter Five

Henry and Cliff ordered takeout from a drive-thru place and wolfed their lunch as they rode in his truck on their way to Sycamore River High School.

"No more, Frito." Cliff yanked away his partially eaten burger from the hungry dog's slobbery mouth. "Mommy will kill me if she finds out I gave you table food."

"Seriously, Cliff?" Henry shook his head as he popped a french fry into his mouth.

Cliff pointed a potato strip at Henry. "I'm still upset with you. You let that poor woman leave the cemetery without getting her contact information. You really should have offered to have her clothing cleaned."

Was this guy serious? "Bro, it was your damn dog that chased her around and demolished that rose she'd been holding. Besides, like I told you already, I offered to have her outfit cleaned, and she just walked away."

He wouldn't dare tell his agent that the woman in the cemetery happened to have been one of his one-nighters. Who needed to listen to more of Cliff's admonishments?

Cliff shook his head. "Not going to look good if she decides to go on social media and tell the tale of how the Hawk wasn't a gentleman."

She had been mortified to lay eyes on him again.

He could see it in her eyes, eyes that looked like amber in the sunlight. Honey-colored eyes.

"You can trust me on this, Cliff. She's not going to blast anything about our encounter on the internet."

"How can you be so sure?"

He needed to get out of this conversation before Cliff started with his interrogation routine. Cliff had a way of sniffing things out.

"I think she had a screw loose."

Cliff snorted. "Why? Because she didn't fawn all over you like those airheads you date?"

"No, because she was talking to a hunk of granite. Like, really having a conversation with a rock."

"It's a cemetery, Henry. That's what you do when you visit a cemetery."

"If you're Beetlejuice."

Cliff blew out a long breath. "How am I going to make the world forget you can be such an asshole?"

"That's why I pay you the big bucks." He deliberately flashed his best smile as he popped another fry into his mouth. "You've got to keep that pooch on a leash when we get to the high school. I don't want him running amuck at my coach's retirement hoopla."

"I'll keep him tethered, and if he gets antsy, I'll take him outside. You know what you're going to say?"

"Yes. I'm going to keep it short and sweet."

"Put a little oomph into it, okay? Sound heartfelt, maybe a little sentimental. Try."

Sycamore River High School was a tall, boxy brick building with big long windows and painted, white double doors. The school looked just as Henry remembered it. The building was first erected in the forties, and since then a couple of additions that jutted out the back had been added. The relatively new gymnasium had its own entrance from the parking lot where Henry parked his SUV.

He slipped a mint into his mouth, cleaned his hands with sanitizer he kept in his glove box, and was ready to go. He couldn't wait for this to be over. Apprehension squeezed his lungs. What if some of these fine folks had seen the latest tabloid stuff about him? Would they even boo him when he stepped up to the podium? God, why had he let Cliff talk him into this?

The bleachers brimmed with students, parents, and faculty. Folding chairs arranged on the hardwood faced the podium, and Henry recognized Coach Lou's wife and his two kids who were not kids anymore. Cliff and his damn dog stood at an open set of doors while Henry went in to find the principal. Thankfully, this principal was new, and the one he had known back in his high school days—the man who reprimanded him many a time and in whose office Henry had sat as punishment for cutting up in some way—was not in attendance.

He shook hands with this new principal, a youngish man about his age, and then took a seat near the podium.

He scanned the crowd for familiar faces. He just didn't want to have to explain himself to these people. This was why he'd put Sycamore River in his rearview mirror. His past belonged in the past. Being here brought up his failings and made him kind of sick. He had to put his foot down about that town anniversary party he'd been invited to. Cliff really wanted him to attend, but this event was about all he could take.

Mr. Adams, the new principal, greeted the crowd and said a few words about Coach Lou. As soon as he mentioned the coach's name, the same old chant from when Henry had been a student here sounded from a group of boys seated together in the bleachers. *Loooooooooo,* they chanted, which almost sounded as if they were booing the guy, but everyone knew it was a loving tribute to how much they appreciated him.

The kids chanting had to be the baseball team. They, like the team he'd been a part of, loved Lou. Everybody loved Coach Lou. Even the scrappy kids, especially the scrappy kids. The kids like he'd been.

When Principal Adams announced him, his body stiffened. All of a sudden, the words he'd had in his head drained out as if a cork had been pulled.

A round of applause filled the room, and somehow Henry managed to push himself up from his chair and make his way up to the podium. Listening to the sounds from the crowd, he detected no booing and surprised himself with how grateful he was for that.

His first few words were too loud, and the microphone made an awkward, thumping sound as he adjusted it to his height. He cleared his throat and thanked everyone for the warm welcome. He felt all the eyes in the room on him; sweat beaded on his forehead, and he hoped it would not drip down his face.

He couldn't remember a single word of what he'd planned to say. He was lucky to remember his own name. What a joke he was to think he'd be able to work for a living as a commentator for major league baseball. He couldn't even form a coherent sentence for a group of townies.

Yet somehow, he pulled it together, the sweat on his brow trickling to his temples. He thanked the coach for all his wisdom and for guiding him through his years as a member of Sycamore River's baseball team. As the words tumbled from his mouth, a voice in the back of his head scoffed at him. *Yeah, right. Coach Lou did such a good job with you that you managed to tank your career right when it was at its peak. Who are you kidding?*

On he went with his sugary words and even managed to recall a story of how Coach Lou told him he'd be a success if he'd just "get out of his own damn way." The crowd laughed. Who wouldn't? The irony was rich.

At last he asked everyone to put their hands together to welcome the man of honor, Coach Lou Brennen. The crowd erupted, and the short bullet of a man came out from the sidelines and joined Henry at the podium.

Coach had aged, his hair steel gray and much thinner on the crown of his head. But behind the frames of his eyeglasses, his eyes were still kind, still true and honest, and when Henry put his hand into Coach's, a lump formed in his throat. This right here was the definition of a good man. All he could say as they were slapping each other on the back was one word. "Coach."

Henry returned to his seat and breathed. Glad his portion was over, he touched the pad of his index finger to his temples to stop the dribble of the sweat anxious to make a beeline down the side of his face.

Coach Lou thanked him, the principal, and everyone in attendance. He professed his undying appreciation to his wife, Janine, and his two kids for being so patient with him throughout his career. When he thanked his team, the boys stood up and chanted

Loooooooo again.

Coach was given an award by the principal, and with a few final words, the presentation was over. People mobbed around him to shake his hand, and although Henry wanted to sneak out a side door, a few kids from the baseball team swarmed him.

"The Hawk!" one boy said. "I can't believe it."

"Hi there."

"Coach wants to see you," another boy said. "Wants to take a picture with you and us."

"Oh." He craned his neck to see Coach looking over at them and giving them a wave of his hand.

"Sure," he said. "Sure."

He went with the kids over to Coach, and this time the man wrapped his arms around Henry and hugged him hard.

"Jeez, it's great to see you, kid." The older man's eyes misted over. "I was so glad you agreed to come to this thing and introduce me. Gotta tell you, at first I wondered if you'd really show up." He chuckled. "I know you."

"Yeah. But how could I turn down a chance to see you, Coach?" He meant it in this moment, even if an hour ago he'd been bitching and moaning for having to be here.

Someone took a photo of them with the team, and then the kids barraged him with questions.

"Henry," Coach said. "The boys would love it if you'd come by on Tuesday and watch them at batting practice. You remember the old batting cages, don't you? We still have them."

"I remember, but, uh, I'm probably going back to New York tonight."

"Please," one of the kids said. "My father says you were the best pitcher who could actually hit and run the bases. Please."

His throat constricted. How to get out of this one? Before he could say anything, Cliff and Frito on a taut leash sauntered over to them.

"Can I get a download of one of those pictures?" Cliff asked the photographer. He turned to Henry. "You're a hit."

"Coach, boys, this is Cliff Jordan, my agent."

"And who's this?" Coach reached down and patted the dog on his head.

"This is Frito," Cliff said. "And he's being a good boy today."

Henry's phone sounded, and he was grateful for the distraction from the question hanging in the air among them. He hated to disappoint Lou, but he couldn't see sticking around an extra couple of days just to see these boys at batting practice.

He eyed the display on his phone and paused at the unfamiliar number.

"Who is it?" Cliff whispered, then motioned his hand. "If you don't know the number, let it go. Don't answer it."

But he did.

"Yes. This is Henry Denhawk."

The female voice was high pitched, and as he listened, he found himself wondering if he'd stopped understanding English. What she was telling him was almost beyond his ability to process.

"Hold on a sec." He turned to Cliff. "Do you have a pen and paper?"

Cliff slapped his pockets, then shook his head.

"I do," one of the boys said and dashed away. In no time he returned with pen and paper.

"Thank you," Henry said. He spoke into the phone again. "Okay, can you repeat that?"

When the call ended, he just stared at his agent.

"Everything okay, Henry?" Coach Lou said, a look of concern on his face.

Henry couldn't find his voice.

"Well?" Cliff's eyes were dark, piercing. "What gives?"

"My stepfather fell in his apartment and broke his hip. And they think he might have had a stroke."

"Sid Goldman?" Coach asked. "Wow, I'm sorry, Henry. Is there anything we can do?"

"Uh, no, Coach. Thanks, but I have to go."

"Sure, sure. You go. Keep in touch."

The men shook hands, and Henry left with Cliff and Frito at his heels.

When they were in the parking lot and sufficiently distanced from others, Cliff hit him on the arm. "You have a stepfather?"

"Sort of."

"What do you mean sort of?"

"We haven't spoken in four years. Not since I ruined my career. We kind of hate each other."

"So why are they calling you?"

Henry was numb. He lifted his shoulders in a shrug. "There's nobody else."

"Where is he?"

"Right here in Sycamore River at the hospital."

Cliff pulled his glasses from his face. A light had come into his beady eyes. "And lovable Henry Denhawk, 'the Hawk,' is going to come to the rescue."

He let out a sarcastic clap of sound. "Sorry, Hank. I don't mean any disrespect, but do you realize the gift you've just been handed?"

Henry closed his eyes. His head throbbed. In his whole life he'd never thought of that grouchy old buzzard, Sidney Goldman, as a gift. "Please stop talking."

"Well, what's the plan?" Cliff sounded as if he were about to salivate. "You going to the hospital?"

"I guess I have to."

"Drop me off downtown. I'll get myself an Uber home. You've got to head to the hospital, and who knows how long you'll be?"

"How are you supposed to get a ride with that behemoth with you?"

"He's a comfort animal. I keep the papers with me for just such scenarios. To deny me and my comfort animal would be discrimination."

He held Cliff's gaze as he started the truck's engine. "You've got an answer for everything."

Cliff grinned. "That's my job. And now you've got your job cut out for you—the dutiful stepson."

"I'm hating this already."

"I'm not."

Chapter Six

"Are you sure it was him?"

Megan cradled the wine glass between her hands and lifted it to her mouth. "Yup."

"What are the chances?" Lucy wagged her head. "I mean, when you have a random hookup, you don't expect to run into the guy, especially in your hometown in a cemetery."

"He wasn't even fazed when he saw me. The whole thing was humiliating." She put the glass down. "I can't drink this. I'm sick over my landlord. The hospital won't tell me anything because I'm not a relative. They said they'd give my contact information to the stepson. I didn't even know Sid had a stepson." She got up from the sofa. "I need a water."

"Hopefully, this stepson will contact you."

She nodded as she went into the kitchen. She pulled a water bottle from the fridge and returned to the living room. She unscrewed the top and guzzled. "I thought seeing the hookup guy was bad, losing the key to my hope chest was bad, but finding my landlord sprawled on the floor like that, I can't get the image out of my head. I'm still shaking."

Lucy reached over and patted her knee. "I know, honey."

"Conjures all kinds of bad memories."

"How could it not? Hey, let's eat. You getting

hungry?"

"Not at all. I'm exhausted. Like this day kicked the crap out of me. I think I'm going to just lie down for a bit." She grabbed her cell phone. "I'd love to hear from Sid's relative that he's okay."

She made her way down the hall to her room and gently closed the door. She flopped onto the bed, knowing sleep would not come. Just closing her eyes, all she could see was the way Sid was sprawled on the tile floor of his kitchen. And when she tried to think of other things, all that came to mind was the guy who had had his mouth and, God help her, other parts of himself all over her that one fateful night and they hadn't known each other from Adam.

One image made her groan. After she and her hookup had sex, he'd run his delicious mouth over the skin of her inner arm, a gentle and slow swath of stimulation. He returned to her wrist, pausing briefly to kiss the shamrock tattoo there, finally stopping to stare at her with those sky-blue eyes.

"My wild Irish rose," he'd said in a sultry tease.

She covered her face with her pillow. *Stop, stop, stop,* her mind implored.

****

Henry dropped Cliff and his dog off for their Uber ride, then drove to the hospital. He pulled his SUV into the parking garage and stopped at the automated ticket station.

After the machine spit the ticket into his grasp, he searched for a parking spot. What was it with all the good spots being saved for *compact cars only*? He cursed under his breath as he went up another aisle. He'd had no business buying such a big vehicle while living in New York, but when money had been no object and every wish had been his command, he'd gone into a dealership and ordered this monster with all the bells and whistles. Now he was stuck with that decision. *Story of my freakin' life.*

Finally finding a corner space that would accommodate his truck, he hopped out and headed to the hospital's entrance. With each step he wondered why he didn't just turn around and go back to his truck. How the hell had he been convinced to come to Sid Goldman's aid? Damn Cliff.

The older lady at the reception desk wore a smock the color of a cantaloupe. With rosy-colored lipstick decorating her lips and her front tooth, she told him Sidney Goldman was in ICU on the second floor.

When he stepped out of the elevator, the corridor to ICU was church quiet. The medicinal zing in the air stung his nostrils and burned his throat. His boots clicked with each step.

He continued to the desk where several workers sat or stood and appeared intense, or maybe he was the one feeling the tension. His nerves raged like he'd chugged a dozen espresso shots. Breathing evenly did not help one single bit. He hadn't laid eyes on his stepfather, and already the guy was messing with him from the inside out.

"Hi." He smiled at the pretty blonde at the desk. Her blue eyes did not send him a cheery welcome, which reminded him he wasn't who he used to be, but at least he saw no recognition in them either. He hated when people knew who he was now, especially after his latest altercation with the dimwit at the bar.

"I'm here to see Sidney Goldman." Was he really

saying those words?

"Are you a relative?"

No how, no way. "He's my stepfather."

She nodded. "Room twenty-four on your left." She lowered her head to resume reading from a clipboard. "But only for a few minutes, okay? Fifteen max."

I'll take ten. No problem.

Sid was tucked tight like a burrito in the bed. His head looked scrawny poking out onto a pillow, his wispy gray hair flyaway like corn silk. His eyes were closed, and his mouth was a seam.

Henry swallowed hard as he approached the bed. A machine on a pole clicked, and a screen flashed digits that seemed to change, like animation, every couple of seconds. Who knew what they meant? A bag of clear liquid dripped through a tube affixed to a fat purple vein in Sid's bony hand. *Shit. Should I say something to him?*

"It's okay to talk to him."

He snapped his head around as if someone had been given access to his inner thoughts. The blue-eyed blonde from the front desk stood in the doorway, a stethoscope slung around her neck. Quite the looker when she smiled like that.

She came deeper into the room, soundlessly on rubber-heeled shoes. "I didn't recognize you at first. You're the Hawk, aren't you?"

Oh boy. Here we go. "Yes, I am, or was, anyway. So how's Sid doing? He just sleeping, or is he in a coma or anything?"

"He's napping. He's weak. They're hoping to get him strong enough for surgery in the morning."

"Surgery?"

"For his hip. They'll put in a metal rod and a prosthetic joint, but so far, we're just getting him stabilized. The doctor should be here soon to talk with you."

"They said they think he also had a stroke?"

"Yes. A moderate ischemic stroke, but I'll let the doctor give you details when you meet with him."

His insides squeezed. "Okay."

"His attending physician is Dr. Brooks, John Brooks. He'll stop in to check on the vitals and consult with Mr. Goldman's orthopedic surgeon. Also, his neurologist, Winifred Harold, will touch base with you. She's the one that can explain everything stroke related. She should be here in about an hour."

An hour? I have to stay here an hour?

"Okay."

"Can I get you anything while you wait?" She batted nice full lashes. "Water? A ginger ale?"

How about some Johnny Walker? I need to get out of here. "Um, is there some place I can buy a cup of coffee?"

"Sure. The cafeteria is on the fifth floor, and there's a coffee shop on the first floor by the gift shop. Your pick."

He slid his gaze over to the burrito in the bed. *Which one is farthest away and will take up more of my time?* "Guess I'll be back in a little while."

"I'm Angie if you need anything."

"Thank you, Angie."

"Wait until I tell my father I've met the Hawk."

Your father? Jeez, I'm an old man. How long before I'm a burrito?

She left, and Henry grabbed his phone to text Cliff

an update, as he'd promised. The man was a shar-pei with a bone. Cliff had badgered him with how he had to play this situation to his advantage, let the world at large see he was a dutiful relative caring for his poor, defenseless stepfather. If the world at large knew that his poor, defenseless stepfather was a troll with a caustic mouth and a nasty streak a mile wide, they wouldn't be so impressed by Henry's bedside visit.

Sid Goldman was no fan of his and vice versa. He'd tolerated the old guy while Mom was alive because for some reason, she loved him. But after his mother's death and Henry's life-altering accident, Sid had lost any ounce of tolerance he had for Henry. The true troll that he was had come out and stayed out. The last thing the old man had said to him was "Get out of my sight." So he had.

Henry had moved to New York City, found a small but upscale apartment on the Upper East Side, and adjusted to life as a has-been. At first, he'd moped around, drunk too much, eaten too much, and watched mindless television. Eventually, though, he'd reached out to a buddy that worked construction, and he'd been hired to do some finishing work. He'd always been good with his hands, and the gig gave him a reason to get up in the morning. He'd put life as a Met, Sycamore River, and the crotchety Sid Goldman in his rearview mirror.

Sid was the quintessential Mets fan. He had Mets crap all over his study—banners, an engraved brick to match the one he had donated to the new Citi Field when they'd built it, a signed Mookie Wilson picture, a couple of autographed baseballs kept in cases. So when Henry had "thrown away" his chance to be part of that team, Sid had lost it. Calling him a loser would have been an endearment compared to the things Sid had spewed.

After texting Cliff, he slipped his phone back in his pocket and headed to the coffee shop. With any luck he'd get stuck in an elevator until visiting hours were over.

Chapter Seven

Henry sat on the hard chair facing the old man in the bed. He sipped the bitter coffee from the paper cup. The three sugars had done nothing to kill the sourness. He'd had the chance to speak to the attending, but he reported what Angie had already told him. He was now waiting to talk to the neurologist. Then he could get the hell out of here.

A middle-aged woman crept into the darkened room and adjusted the lighting to slightly brighten the space. Henry didn't like the way Sid looked in the new light. His face was gray, his eyelids veiny and flimsy-looking, like tissue paper. He turned away from the sight of the old man and met the woman's gaze. She had kind eyes, eyes like his mother's.

"Mr. Denhawk, hello. I'm Winifred Harold, your father's neurologist."

"Stepfather."

"Excuse me?"

The puzzled look on her face might have been from the abruptness of his correction. He cleared his throat. "Sid is my stepfather. Nice to meet you, Doctor."

She put a hand to his shoulder before she went to Sid. She took his pulse, touched a delicate hand to his forehead. She consulted his chart. She studied the blipping machine next to him.

"How, uh, is he?"

"He's been through a lot, but he's stronger than he looks. Strong heart."

He wanted to laugh. Sid Goldman had a strong heart because it was made out of cement.

"Your stepfather should be going in for the hip tomorrow morning. Has Doctor Marshall talked with you?"

"Not yet."

"He'll be here soon, I'm sure." She tilted her head as she met Henry's gaze. "I'm glad you're here for him. There will be some decisions to be made."

Decisions? He put the coffee cup on the tray table beside the bed. The cooling bitter liquid churned his stomach.

"Depending on how well he does postsurgery, we should be sending him to a rehab facility soon afterward. Do you have a preference as to which facility?"

"Um, no, I don't. I mean, are there more than one in Sycamore River?"

She smiled. "One is in Sycamore River, and the other is in Morristown. Both are fine places, but I'd suggest Oak Manor, which is here in town. That way it will be more convenient for you to visit him each day."

Visit him each day? How the hell was he supposed to come and see this guy every day? Would the old buzzard even want to see his face at all, let alone be in constant company? *Oh cripes, this is getting out of hand.*

The doctor patted Henry's shoulder. "As soon as you speak with Dr. Marshall, you should go get some rest. He'll tell you what time to come here in the morning for Sidney's surgery, if he goes in. We'll talk some more then." She stepped away then stopped to look back. "Good night. Get some sleep tonight."

After she was gone, he eyed the old man. The papery lids were still closed; his mouth was dry and pale. This sucked. Henry slowly lifted himself from the chair and went to get his jacket.

"Putz."

He snapped his head around.

Sidney Goldman had opened his eyes, and his pale mouth was a sideways slash of disdain. "Huh, at least you know your name." His voice was gravelly, harsh, yet just above a whisper.

Ignoring the man's gibe, Henry approached the bed tentatively. "Maybe I should call a nurse or something."

"For what?"

"I don't know. To let them know you're awake."

"Rocket scientist."

He found Sid's call button and pressed it. "A nurse should be here any minute."

"What are you doing here?"

"They called me. They, uh, found my name and number in your wallet."

Sid attempted to snicker, but the sound was a raggedy screech. "How long are you here for?"

"Well, I guess that depends on you."

A nurse came into the room and went straight to Sid's bedside. "Mr. Goldman, hello there," she chirped. She ran a gentle hand over his flyaway hair. "How are you feeling?"

"Ducky."

She turned to Henry. "You've got the magic touch, it seems."

He smiled as if what she said made sense, but all

he could think was that if he were magic, he'd make himself disappear about now.

Dr. Marshall, a broad and hefty man, came in and gave Sid a going-over. Finally, he turned to Henry. "Your father is good to go for surgery tomorrow morning. Eight o'clock."

"He's my stepfather."

The doctor's eyes stared at him behind black-rimmed glasses.

"I guess I'll see you in the morning, then, Sid." The words tasted metallic and were awkward on his tongue.

Sid perked up. "Go to my place."

Aware of the others in the room, Henry did his best to lighten his voice, infuse it with some warmth. "Um, Sid, that's very nice, but I think I'll just grab a room at the Admiral."

"I'm not being hospitable. I need you to take care of Mookie."

"Who?"

"My cat. He's on medication and can't miss a dose. The bottle's on the kitchen counter."

He felt the eyes of the nurse and doctor on him. "Sure, sure, I can do that."

"Keys are in my jacket."

His voice was starting to fade, and he seemed strained, the tendons in his neck taut and garish.

"Relax, Sid. I'll take care of it." He fished the keys out of the pocket of the jacket stored in the narrow closet. "I understand."

"No back door. Go through the store."

"I thought the camera store closed."

"New owner," Sid rasped. "She's a nice lady. Leave her alone."

With the two sets of eyes still on him, he proffered a smile he did not feel. "Glad you're feeling better, Sid. I'll see you tomorrow."

On his way to the elevator, he was stopped by a nurse at the front desk who handed over a slip of paper.

"This is the woman who found your stepfather. She's anxious to hear how he's doing. If you have a minute, she'd appreciate a phone call."

"Thank you." He shoved the paper into his back pocket.

He was tired, cranky, and in need of a beer. He was too wiped to go to a bar, so he stopped off and picked up a sub sandwich and a six-pack and headed to Sid's apartment. It was the last place he wanted to go. He'd walked out of that residence four years ago and hadn't looked back. He just wanted his own bed in his own apartment in the city. Wasn't happening. Not tonight anyway.

He couldn't wait to jump in a hot shower and wash off this day.

****

Sid's apartment looked as if it had been frozen in time. The pillows his mother cross-stitched were still on the old burgundy sofa, and the same candy dish—empty now instead of brimming with butterscotch—sat on the coffee table.

Henry put down his sandwich and pulled a beer from the six-pack before shoving the carton into the fridge. The kitchen was the same as well. The rooster wallpaper, the Formica countertops, the huge double porcelain sink.

He popped open the beer and took a long pull. The crisp, cool beverage slid down easily. He went to the door, picked up his duffle, and made his way into the room down the hall that had been his bedroom once upon a time. He stopped at the doorway to the other bedroom that had sat undisturbed like a shrine for so many years. Andrew's room.

He'd only dared to go into the space when no one was around. Now, alone and free of anyone showing up, he stepped into the room. The maple bedroom set, the plaid quilt on the bed, the shelf on the wall brimming with junior high and high school accomplishments. Second place in a spelling contest in seventh grade, Most Improved Player from his eighth-grade varsity baseball team. That was after Andrew had been diagnosed with the blood disorder that made him so tired and weak.

Andrew's participation trophy from his junior varsity baseball team from freshman year of high school stood prominently in the middle of the shelf. How proud that kid had been of all this stuff, and forget Sid. To him, these tokens were probably as important as a World Series trophy. He snickered into the cool, silent space. If he'd have won the World Series as a Met, that achievement wouldn't have impressed Sid as much as this wall of gold-tone tin.

Sid's son's death had taken a toll on Sid and Henry's mother, too. Sid had never been the same after Andrew died. He'd developed a darkness, an anger, a deep-seated resentment, and Henry had been the recipient.

God, it came flooding back. Sports had come naturally to him, while poor Andrew worked doggedly to keep a place on his school team. But Sid had blamed him, hated him for his abilities, and after Henry's accident, well, Sid couldn't even look at him. It had never been said aloud, but Henry knew as well as Sid that the old man's resentment went so deep, dark enough for him to believe the wrong young man had died.

He left the room and went to the one that had been his. Unsurprisingly, the twelve-foot square had been wiped clean of anything that identified the space as his. No awards were displayed on the walls, no photos, no banners. But there was a bed, and it was made, and he couldn't wait to take a shower, enjoy his Italian sub and another beer, and then hit the sack. He downed the beer in his hand, placed the empty bottle on the nightstand, no coaster, and stripped out of his clothing. He couldn't wait to wash off this day.

Chapter Eight

Megan lay sprawled on her bed and channel surfed with no success. Nothing good was on TV tonight. Nothing to hold her interest and keep her mind occupied.

If she went to bed this early, she'd never sleep. All she could think about was what happened with Sid Goldman and how his big orange cat was all alone tonight.

She'd given the animal water and food before she left Sid's apartment, and she'd cleaned up the spilled chardonnay and the broken glass. But she worried that Mookie would be wondering where his owner was. What if something happened to the poor animal? Mookie had a condition that required medication. What if he missed a dose?

She didn't know why she felt so responsible for the fluff ball, but somehow, she did. Was it her duty to watch over Mookie until Sid came home? *If he came home*. She closed her eyes to banish the errant thought. She didn't know her landlord very well, but she shared a kinship with the old gent who enjoyed inviting her for cocktails and some conversation. Maybe it was their mutual widowed state. She didn't know. Guilt for her begrudging acceptance of his last invite seeped into her bones. An image of how she'd found him taunted her brain. *Please don't die, Sid.*

She wouldn't sleep tonight until she knew Mookie was okay. Groaning, she flung off her nightclothes and tugged on a running suit, jabbed her feet into slip-on sneakers. She turned off the television. Lucy was in the shower, so she jotted a quick note on a sticky pad, grabbed her jacket and purse, and left in pursuit of easing her mind.

Downtown, Megan parked her compact SUV in front of the store. She went inside and took in the space, dark except for a dim beam from the streetlamp outside the front window. Her wares were in shadow, appearing like a mishmash of angles. *So much to do.* A trickle of doubt dripped into her veins. She promised herself she'd be open for Halloween when all the stores downtown hosted a kind of open-house event, giving away candy and welcoming kids and their parents. It would be the perfect opportunity to have the Hope Chest become an official part of the community. She straightened her stance. Doubt did not belong here. Her shop was the one thing she had control of—at least that was how she felt tonight.

She needed the shop to open on time and pushed away the doubt that crept into her head. Available funds were running thin, but that wouldn't stop her. Before she met William, she'd spent her life making one piddly diner paycheck along with her tips last until the next payday. She knew how to survive during a financial drought, which right now was temporary while she pursued her life's dream. She'd let nothing stand in her way of being her own woman who had her own place on the map.

She crossed the room, her steps echoing on the old wooden floorboards, and unlocked the door to the back vestibule. Climbing the staircase up to Sid's door, she forced the scene from earlier out of her mind. Seeing his cat would make her feel good, feel useful. *Okay, Mookie, here I come.*

She stepped into the apartment, low lit by a table lamp in the corner, and Mookie darted from the hallway to greet her. His plume-like tail shot straight up and did a little quirky wiggle.

"Hello, kitty," Megan cooed. Her heart squeezed. She felt better already.

The cat dropped to the rug like a bag of sand and rolled onto his back. Megan crouched and gave the cat's tummy a good rub. "How's your food bowl, kitty?"

She grabbed the bag of cat food from the dining room table and turned to walk toward the kitchen, her breath hitching as she fought against the image of Sid sprawled in that peculiar way.

A noise stopped her, then the prickle of gooseflesh rose on her skin. She was not alone. She knew it. Her heart rate quickened. Had she stumbled upon a burglary? Her lungs suffered for air.

She turned around slowly, her breath trapped in her throat. A man, a hulky man with blondish hair, stood in front of her wearing nothing but a white terry bath towel knotted at his waist. She screamed so loud Mookie hopped a foot off the ground, then dashed away.

"Calm down." The man took a step in her direction, hands up in the air.

Her gaze shot down to the precarious-looking fold of fabric at his waist. Her gaze shot back up to his face. Dear God, this could not be happening. It was him again, the hookup guy. What on earth was he doing in Sid's apartment? Was this some kind of cruel joke? She didn't know this man, although she'd lain naked with him. He could be a robber or a murderer or a kidnapper. What did she know about him besides every single contour of his bare flesh?

"Don't come any closer." She held up the bag of cat food as though it were a shield. "What are you doing here? And why are you wet?"

"Okay, first off I'm Sid's stepson, and secondly, we're old friends by now, aren't we, Megan?"

His gaze locked on hers, and that devilish smile claimed his lips. The snake was enjoying this. Ire trickled through her veins at the thought of this man showing up time and again to remind her of her failure at one-night stands.

"*You're* Sid's stepson? You've got to be kidding me."

His sky-blue eyes took her in from head to toe, her skin reacting in an outbreak of gooseflesh. His gaze landed on the tattoo on her wrist peeking out from the sleeve of her jacket. She quickly tugged down the fabric to hide the telltale tat, heat climbing up her face.

That sexy crooked smile wooed her with its claim of his lips, the kind of smile he'd used the night she lost her ever-loving mind. "The Irish rose."

She swallowed hard. "You didn't answer. You're Sid's stepson?"

"Sorry." He took a step in her direction to which she jumped back as if someone had tossed a lit firecracker at her face. He froze in place. "Yes, Sid was married to my mother."

"Oh." Her eyes couldn't help but take him in, the

broad shoulders, the smooth, taut skin of his torso. She knew just how that skin felt to her fingertips, and she breathed in deeply, letting the air escape in a slow hiss.

"First the cemetery and now this," he said, so clearly amused she wanted to slap that look off his face, only she'd have to touch him, and God only knew what she'd do if she dared.

"What are the chances, huh?"

"Yeah, well." She put the bag of cat food down and eyed the two bowls that sat on a mat on the floor. "I came by to check on Mookie. I didn't want him to be scared that Sid's not here."

"Nice of you."

"How is Sid?"

"Not great. He definitely had a stroke—a rather moderate one, I'm told—but nonetheless. So they're monitoring him before they schedule surgery for a new hip."

"I hope he'll be okay."

"We'll see."

"Has he been awake?"

"Oh yeah. He was awake when I was there."

"Will you tell him I'm thinking about him?"

"Of course." The lazy smile angled on his face again.

"Did you, uh, give Mookie his medicine? He needs to take it every night."

"Yes. He's all set."

"Okay, good."

"So, Megan, you're Sid's tenant. You're the one who found him."

"Yes."

"The doctor told me your quick action was why

he's still with us."

Her face flushed. She hadn't felt as if she'd done anything brave when she summoned paramedics to Sid's aid. She'd felt unhinged. And this blast from her recent past was not helping one bit.

She raised her chin to this tall, nearly naked man who glistened in the lamplight. Something inside her—a deep, secretive part of herself, a part with no conscience—thumped rhythmically, like a mating drum.

"Megan Harris, right?" They hadn't shared last names on that fateful night. "The nurse at the hospital gave me your contact information. I was, uh, going to call you after I cleaned up and had a bite to eat."

"I see." She tried to look away but couldn't. His skin was dewy, and her fingers, with a mind of their own, itched to just reach out and touch him, feel him. Why was he tan in October? His skin looked sun kissed. His hair was more gold than blond, his nose sharp, his eyes wide-set and compelling. Her eyeballs were no friend to her at the moment.

"My full name's Henry Denhawk, in case you didn't know."

He'd told her his name was Henry on the night in New York, but that had been all she knew. The formality of last names hadn't been necessary. She was more ashamed at this moment than she'd been before. She had to get out of here.

Henry Denhawk tilted his head. "Although the circumstances are far from ideal, it's nice to see you again, Megan Harris." He took another small step in her direction, and he extended his hand. In the effort the towel around his waist slipped down his frame just an inch, one daring little inch.

She audibly sucked in her breath, then shouted, "Grab that towel!"

He reached for the towel and held it from falling totally away from his body. For a millisecond she relished the idea of getting a glimpse to see if her memory of his contours was accurate or just her mind playing grandiose tricks on her.

"Wait here," he said. "I'm going to throw some clothes on."

As he walked away, her eyes took in the vision of his broad shoulders, the muscles taut. Was he a weightlifter? Her gaze slid down to the towel that hugged his butt. The terry cloth only accented his rump's spectacular silhouette. She remembered. He was the guy on the paper towel package come to life and dipped in gold.

The only good thing about her thoughts was that they proved she wasn't dead inside. Some days she had her doubts. Ever since William died, she'd written off the idea of another man, had been blind to them. Well, help her, Lord, but she was no longer blind. *Now I see!* She squeezed her eyes closed.

She busied herself with refilling Mookie's water bowl. The faucet leaked, and despite her wiggling the handle, the steady droplets would not stop. Did the shower faucet drip as well, and had the golden man down the hall fiddled with it as he stood all shiny and wet under the spray of water? She needed to knock this stuff off. She eyed the steady, unrelenting stream of water droplets. Her brain and that damn faucet had something in common—both were faulty and could use a good twist from a wrench.

She heard him come into the room. She smelled him, too. His scent was clean, fresh, and Paul Bunyan-outdoorsy. Pine maybe.

He wore faded blue jeans that hugged his frame. He was tucking in a blue plaid shirt, and fascinated, she watched his hand as it continually dipped into the waistband of the jeans. Tuck, tuck, tuck. Lord Almighty, she had to stop.

Say something. "The faucet leaks." *Brilliant, Megan.*

"Yes. I see that." He took a step in her direction, and she willed her immune system to kick in and cancel out the unbidden effect of this lumberjack.

"I, uh, brought over my rent check earlier, when I, you know, found Sid." She took a step backward. "It was on the dining room table. Did you find it?"

"No, but I'll take a look."

He has to be over six two. "Great."

"I'm going to the hospital in the morning, and I'll let Sid know you delivered the check."

His eyes were cornflower blue, she decided. "Thank you. And please let him know I'm saying my prayers."

"No problem."

The faucet in her brain needed more than a twist from a wrench to stop the constant trickle of outlandish thoughts. *Who has eyes that color? How old is he? His hair looks nice damp like that with rake marks from a comb.*

"I'm glad Mookie has company." She offered a smile. *See? I'm not crazy.* She breathed, then tried to sound casual. "So I'm glad he's got you." She inched toward the doorway. "I guess I'll be going, then."

She didn't know how to maneuver around the guy without touching him, although something in her betraying brain dared her to do just that. Henry Denhawk filled the doorway, filled the room, and his smell filled her nostrils.

"Wait a second, Megan."

Oh, she liked the way her name sounded on his lips. *Bad, bad, bad.*

"Yes?" The word came out in a whisper.

"I wanted to apologize for what happened at the cemetery. For the record, that dog isn't mine. He belongs to my agent."

This guy had an agent? What did he do? She couldn't help it. Her gaze traveled over his big body. Maybe he modeled for some kind of big-boy clothing or something.

"I'd still like to pay for your dry cleaning."

She had to try to get past him, contorting her body as if avoiding a flame. "That's, uh, not necessary."

"I'll stop by your store tomorrow to let you know how Sid's doing."

Oh Lord. She didn't want to see him again, but she couldn't very well tell him not to bother. "Great."

She left the apartment, left the building, and sat in her car with her hands squeezed tight at ten and two. She needed to go to confession or, better yet, to Gate of Heaven Cemetery to confess her sin at William's headstone. She hoped the way she shivered was because of the cool night and not the way that specimen's blue eyes studied her almost as if he had X-ray vision and could read her thoughts like newsprint.

All the way home she stared straight ahead at the road while breathing in and out like the women on TV did when they were in labor. Whatever she was giving birth to scared the bejesus out of her.

Chapter Nine

"Your hookup is the Hawk?" Lucy's eyes were big and incredulous. "You've got to be kidding."

"Who?"

"Henry Denhawk, you know, the Hawk, from the Mets. The hometown bad boy who caused a scandal back a few years ago."

A scandal? Her mind zoomed. What the heck was Lucy talking about?

"Here, look." Lucy, who was sitting at the kitchen table with her laptop, clicked away at her keyboard. "You've got to remember this about the guy."

She turned the screen toward Megan. There was a photo of Henry with that signature lopsided grin and his dashingly handsome face. Above his picture was the headline, "Once a Bad Boy."

"What's this?" Her voice was a whisper.

"Read."

She scanned the article, then clicked onto another page and saw that for four years straight Henry Denhawk had done nothing right. He'd gotten into bar fights, been reckless on a ski slope, and almost died as a result. He'd lost his contract with the Mets and for the last four years was doing who knew what. Most recently he had been involved in a tiff with some guy in a bar in the city. Words had been exchanged, and a fistfight had ensued. Her heart turned to granite. This guy was a louse.

"Wow." She plunked down onto a chair at the table. "When it comes to one-night stands, I sure can pick 'em."

"How could you know? He was there, all pretty and flirty, and you were just tipsy enough, and there you have it. Don't think twice about it."

"But I do, Lucy. I'm ashamed as it is, and now that I know what kind of guy I'm dealing with, I'm even more mortified. This is why I should never listen to my own whims. I'm more logical than that." She covered her face with her hands. "And he's in town for God only knows how long now that Sid's not well. Right above my store, no less. Just steps away. Does this sound like a cruel joke to you? Because it sure does to me."

"It's interesting. I'll say that much."

"I feel sick."

"Oh, come on, Megs. It's not that bad."

She ran down the hallway to the bathroom and retched into the bowl. Her head spun. She'd wanted to feel alive again. *Well, welcome to the living, Megan.* And she got sick one more time.

Chapter Ten

Henry sat in the waiting room and stared at the pale green tile floor. He could tell which tiles had been replaced because the green was just a little off.

The doctor had said the operation typically took around two and a half hours, but they wouldn't know for sure until they were working on Sid.

The room was a large square with walls painted that sickening tone of green. Several others waited, too, hoping for good news about their loved ones. Just the idea of Sid Goldman being a "loved one" made him cringe. Even at their best, the two men had merely tolerated each other. No love had linked them other than that they had both loved Henry's mom.

He watched the electronic board on the long wall that was coded with information on how all procedures were going. Sid was still in the operation.

He tried reading the newspaper someone had left on a table, tried to go through emails on his phone, but he was preoccupied. Thoughts of Megan Harris would not relent.

His mouth automatically curved into a smile as he imagined her face when she'd seen him in the towel. Skittish like a colt. He hadn't meant to startle the woman. He couldn't believe he had run into her in two places in his hometown. The time they spent together that night in the city hadn't revealed she had a connection to Sycamore River.

He thought of the shamrock tattoo on her delicate wrist. He'd never forget the way she'd offered the wrist up to him as he kissed the image, then continued his kissing up her soft, milky-skinned upper arm. How could he forget?

Megan Harris was anything but forgettable. He'd keep his mouth shut about it, but Cliff would buy him a cigar if he knew he'd had a one-nighter with a woman like Megan. First off, she was well past college age, and the word *like* didn't insert itself into all her sentences. He hated to admit it now, but Cliff had been right about the ladies he'd spent time with over the past few years. They'd been time fillers, distractions from his otherwise disappointing life. Young women whose names he could not recollect now.

He didn't know anything about Megan other than she had a luscious body and an unabashed way of enjoying physical pleasure. Also, he presumed she must like cats because whenever Sid's cat, Mookie, would come near her, she'd raise her voice into a high, childlike lilt and talk to it as if it were somebody's baby. Again, his mouth slid into a grin, and it confused him. He liked women. A lot. But this Megan was the unlikeliest of women he would approach for a date or someone he'd chat up in a bar. He had a kind of radar when it came to the female persuasion, and this one had dangerous things written all over her, things like picket fences and weddings and babies even. Not for him. No way.

Cliff warned him to swear off dating the typical too-skinny, vapid young women he charmingly referred to as "tits on a stick." Now he chuckled to himself.

What would his agent think of this brunette with the soft brown eyes and the obviously natural curves, especially if he found out she was the woman from the cemetery?

Henry thought of her holding up that bag of cat food as if it were a weapon, her demand that he identify himself. He chuckled again, then wiped the stupid smile from his mouth.

Megan Harris seemed like a good, stable person who had a thing or two to say about what was on her mind. She seemed as though she had a nose for bullshit and could readily pick up its scent. Her eyes, the color of sweet tea, were filled with intelligence and yet a kind of vulnerability. Sadness maybe? *Shit*. Thinking about her had been fun when he thought of her jumpiness around his terry loincloth. But no good would come from having thoughts of her in a more serious vein.

If he knew what was good for him—and he was trying to do just that these days—he'd steer clear of her. He'd been the king of bullshit with women because it was just easier to be on his own for the long haul. Starting up anything with Megan would be a disaster. Besides, he was only in Sycamore River until Sid stabilized.

The orthopedist, Dr. Marshall, in blue scrubs and booties, came into the waiting room and called out to him. He jumped up from his seat, suddenly nervous about what the man might say.

"He did well." The doctor patted him on the shoulder. "He's in recovery now and should be in his room in a couple of hours."

"Okay. Uh, thank you."

Dr. Marshall nodded and turned to leave. Henry

left the room, snaked his way through the corridors, and boarded an elevator. He breathed deeply, glad the old man had made it through the operation.

In his truck he called Cliff to fill him in.

"Good news," Cliff said. "And in keeping with the good news thing, I got a call from Roger Dennis. They want to meet with you on Friday."

"They do? What's this mean, Cliff?"

"I think it means they're keeping an eye on you—thanks to me, I might add—and they've noticed you're being a Boy Scout these days. He saw the picture of you at the cemetery and the one with you and your good old baseball coach from school. I told you they'd eat that stuff up. Why don't you post something on social media about how glad you are the old man made it through his operation? Thank people for their thoughts and prayers. You know, that kind of stuff."

"Absolutely not."

"Why do you make this so difficult, Hank? Just play the goddamn game, would you?"

He was sick of games. Did it have something to do with his nearing the big four-oh? Or maybe the sight of Sid Goldman wrapped up like a fragile burrito in a hospital bed when four years ago he'd been a vibrant little jerk? Whatever, the idea of thanking people for prayers he himself did not ask for just seemed wrong.

"Friday at ten in the morning," Cliff interrupted Henry's thought process. "I'll meet you there at nine so we can game-plan before we meet with them."

He grabbed an egg sandwich from the coffee shop in Sycamore River and wondered what he'd do with the couple of hours before he had to go back to the hospital to check on Sid.

He found himself driving in the direction of the old batting cages. He'd sworn he wouldn't get involved, that it made no sense whatsoever considering he was heading back to New York the minute he was able. But that was just where he went.

He parked his truck in the gravel lot and looked across the field where the boys on the team, Coach Lou, and some other adult male congregated.

He made his way slowly to the cages, second-guessing his decision to show his face. But Coach invariably spotted him and waved his clipboard high in the air.

"There he is!" The enthusiasm in his voice gave Henry a pang of guilt for the "oh no" he thought when Coach first saw him. He waved back.

Soon he was surrounded by the boys, who all talked above each other, and he couldn't decipher a thing they were saying. All he knew was that they were glad as hell to see him. He couldn't help it; he laughed.

He watched the batters, instinctively gave some bits of advice. "Choke up," he said. "Follow through. Rip it."

"Thanks for coming, Hank. The boys appreciate it, and it means a lot to me. How's Sid?"

"He had the operation on his hip this morning. It went well. Waiting now for him to get out of recovery and into his room. I had a little time and thought I'd come by and see what was going on with you and your team."

"You remembered that we practice Tuesdays and Thursdays." Coach smiled. "That's great."

"You've got some good hitters."

"We do."

The other man with him was in the dugout with the boys.

"Who's that?"

"He's new. Bill Lloyd. He's one of the math teachers and is filling in until they find my replacement."

"How about him? Doesn't he want the job?"

Coach Lou shook his head and grimaced. "He's got a lot to learn. Nice guy—don't get me wrong—but he's got to toughen up. He knows the game. I'll give him that much. But coaching is something different. Ideally, I'd wish for someone more hands on, a down-in-the-dirt kind of guy. Someone who, I don't know, walked in these boys' shoes. Know anyone?"

Henry chuckled. "You could use a lesson in subtlety. I'm not going to be available. As a matter of fact, I have a meeting with the Mets later this week for a commentator position. My agent's optimistic."

"Wow, good for you, Hank. Is that what you're hoping for?"

"Of course. Why wouldn't I?"

Coach Lou shrugged. "Never pictured you in that type of role. You know, a talking head. You're more of an action guy."

Henry laughed. "Believe me. I'm looking forward to being one of their talking heads. If you can't play…"

"You teach."

"Or you analyze. That's what I'm betting on."

A tall, straight-as-an-arrow-looking boy whose expression broadcasted he was aggravated about something approached Coach Lou. Henry invented that look.

"Am I getting time in the cages today or what?" he

asked in a belligerent tone Henry unfortunately recognized.

Coach, unfazed, shrugged. "If there's time."

The kid groaned and walked away, kicking dirt as he went back to the bleachers.

"A charmer, I'll bet," Henry said with a laugh.

"Takes one to know one, huh, Hank?"

"Why, Coach, I have no idea what you're talking about."

Coach Lou laughed, a good hearty sound, and Henry was reminded just how much he liked this guy. What he saw was what he got from this man who had been there for him for the four years he'd played for the Sycamore River Tigers.

He met the first- and second-string pitchers, both good ballplayers. The younger boy, Joshua, a skinny kid with long arms and legs, showed raw talent and assuredness beyond his years. Henry gave the two kids a couple of pointers, bits of wisdom, but soon made his exit. He didn't want Coach to get too comfortable seeing him with the team. Coaching kids wasn't in his cards. He and major league baseball might have a date with destiny, and he was ready.

****

The walk to the diner cleared Megan's head. While she'd been working at the shop, she'd felt a bit dizzy, and when she realized it was after noon, she thought she'd go for a nice bowl of homemade soup.

She ran into candy shop owners Joe and Elaine, who were outside decorating their front window with pumpkin and scarecrow decals.

"How's the store coming?" Elaine waved.

"Getting there."

"Looking forward to browsing," she said, and her husband gave her a look of mock distress.

"There goes our bank account," he gibed.

"Will we see you at the town anniversary party?" Elaine asked.

"Depends on how I do with the store. I really want to put my time into opening on Halloween."

"Fingers crossed."

She bid them goodbye and continued on her jaunt to the diner. She loved this stretch of Main Street. The shops were eclectic and inviting. The Hope Chest would be in fine company. When William was alive, they hadn't taken the time to enjoy Sycamore River's downtown. He was always working, and she hadn't felt as if she belonged. It wasn't until she'd randomly met Lucy at Java Joe's that she finally made her own friend. Everyone else she'd associated with had been through William's work acquaintances or the wives of William's friends from the country club. She sucked at golf and hadn't ever felt like putting in the time to get better at it. After William's death, she'd let the membership lapse and was just as glad.

She enjoyed the cool air that ruffled through her hair and brushed over her face. She closed her eyes in appreciation.

The diner was crowded at midday, and she took a seat at the counter. The familiar waitress, Betty, a middle-aged woman with salt-and-pepper hair fashioned in a bun, greeted her.

She ordered a cup of tea and a bowl of their homemade vegetable barley soup. One taste and she was in heaven.

"Megan?"

She turned to the voice. Carolyn Montgomery stood there in her golf wear, raspberry-pink shorts and a white-collared shirt trimmed in raspberry-toned piping. Her blonde ponytail poked out from the back of her coordinating visor.

She'd forgotten that the diner was a frequent pit stop for those done for the day with their golf games. How many times had she crammed herself into a booth with three other women who ordered seltzers with lemon and salad with dressing on the side while she ordered herself a BLT?

"Hi, Carolyn." Megan put her spoon down and waited. The woman never just said hello.

Back when she and William belonged to the golf club, she and Carolyn had played foursomes with two other women from town, women who also dressed in their finest golf attire purchased at the sports boutique that had gone in at the new hotel downtown.

Those women enjoyed the game or at least did a good job pretending they did. Megan had never felt a part of their little group, and their conversations between holes were most often shrouded in gossip. The whispered comments stoked vulnerability in her as though the moment she wasn't in their company she would be the topic of their snarky commentary.

Carolyn's husband, Fritz, had been one of William's colleagues at work, and they had often carpooled into the city each day or sat together on the train. They'd frequently gone to dinner with Carolyn and Fritz, had them over for barbecues in the summer, and had gone on a long weekend to Mystic Seaport in Connecticut one fall.

After Megan quit the golf club, her connection to

Carolyn and the other ladies of that golf world had faded away. She didn't miss it one bit.

"What have you been doing with yourself?" Carolyn said as though Megan owed her some kind of explanation of her comings and goings. "And is what I hear true?"

Megan's chest muscles cinched into a shield. *Here we go.* God only knew what Carolyn might have heard. She looked at her, knowing it wouldn't be long before she spilled what she was alluding to.

"I was surprised to learn that you're soon to be among the merchants here in town. Janice told me she'd heard you're opening up a dollar store. Is that really happening?" She laughed as though she found the news to be absurd.

"No," Megan said, doing her best not to sound off putting. "It's a thrift shop that I'm opening."

"A thrift shop? You mean like an indoor yard sale?"

She opened her mouth to say something but closed it again. Her soup was getting cold.

"Anyway," Carolyn said with a laugh, "I'm glad to have run into you." She pulled her phone out of a small cross-body purse, pressed some keys, and flipped through screens with her thumb. "Right." She looked up. "You haven't RSVP'd about the dinner dance. You are coming, I hope."

Of course, Carolyn was involved in the event. Megan hadn't decided on attending, and although she knew it would be good PR for her to show her face, she just didn't think she had it in her. Returning to that hunter-green and beige ballroom would bring back too many memories, memories of the days of pretending to enjoy the company and the festivities, times when she even wondered how it was that she and William were a couple in the first place. Although they loved each other, they had next to nothing in common.

"We miss you, Megan."

She met Carolyn's gaze. The woman sounded sincere, but Megan couldn't help wondering if she was just turning on that earnest tone as though it came from the flow of a faucet.

"Please say you'll come. All the store owners will be there."

Attending this dinner made sense. As a shopkeeper, she'd have the chance to meet the others and make connections. She eyed Carolyn, whose gaze was locked on her.

"I'm sorry, Carolyn. I just haven't decided yet. It will depend if I can spare the time. But, uh, thank you for including me."

"Of course," Carolyn cooed. "We love you."

That was another thing about Carolyn. She loved everything.

Betty came out from the kitchen with a large bag filled with wrapped menu items.

"Oh, Betty, thank you. You're a doll," Carolyn said, her tone coated in syrupy appreciation.

"Hi, there," a voice came from behind her.

Henry Denhawk stood there with his hands in his jean pockets, the collar to his windbreaker turned up. Sunglasses rested on his head.

"Hi," Megan responded, glad for the distraction from Carolyn.

Carolyn batted her lashes at him. "Oh, I know who you are," she cooed. "Everyone's talking about the fact that the Hawk is back in town." She extended a hand, bent at the wrist. "Carolyn Montgomery."

He took her hand and flashed her one of his winning smiles. *Oh brother.* Megan picked up her cup of tea and took a sip. Cold.

"My son, Joshua, is one of the pitchers for the Sycamore River Tigers. He said you came down to watch the team practice batting. He was thrilled to meet you and said you gave him some good pointers."

"I remember Joshua. He's got a good arm."

The woman beamed. Megan wondered if the way she batted her eyes would make her lashes fall off. Carolyn fiddled with her cell phone, looking intently at the screen, then her head shot up.

"Say, Henry, I'm so delighted that you'll be joining us at the anniversary dinner. I just checked to see that you RSVP'd as a yes. We're all so pleased our very own local celebrity will be in attendance."

"Yes, but keep in mind that my schedule could change due to my stepfather's medical situation."

"Of course." She waved a dismissive hand in Megan's direction. "We're still hoping Megan can spare the time to attend. She's in the midst of opening up a store of sorts."

A store of sorts. Megan wanted to fish out a carrot from her soup and fling it in Carolyn's face.

"It's a big undertaking. You know, starting up a business." Henry's gaze momentarily flashed to greet Megan's.

"Oh, I'm sure," Carolyn said as she touched his arm with a delicate hand. "Megan, we hope to see you. And, Henry, it goes without saying that your relative's wellness is your priority, but it would be lovely to have you join us for the commemorative event. Here's my business card in case you have any questions."

He accepted the card while Megan rested her elbow on the counter and supported her head with her hand. His eyes twinkled with amusement.

"Thank you, Carolyn."

As much as Megan detested the scene, she did get a kick out of the way Carolyn seemed to unravel when the famous Hawk said her name. *Ridiculous.*

As Carolyn left the diner, Henry took a seat on the stool next to Megan.

"How is Sid?" She watched him flag the waitress, and just a hand gesture gave the cue for her to pour him a cup of coffee. Apparently, this wasn't his first time in this establishment.

"He made it out of surgery okay, and he's out of recovery and in his room. I'm heading back later."

"I'm glad to hear the news." She lifted her mug to take a sip of her tea and thought better of it.

"You didn't eat your soup," he commented.

"Yeah." She made a face. "It's gotten cold. Missed my window."

The waitress brought him a mug of coffee and leaned forward on the counter in front of him. "Can I get you something to eat?"

"How about a grilled cheese and a cup of that soup." He pointed to Megan's lunch. "And could you do us a favor and warm hers up?"

"Sure, doll," she said as she took away Megan's bowl.

"You didn't have to do that." She paused. "But thank you."

"Well, now you don't have to miss that window.

What you wanted you can still enjoy. All you have to do is ask." He flashed her a smile. "Keep that in mind."

Her heart did a little jig in her chest. This big blond ballplayer was pretty damn fresh. Heat climbed up her cheeks.

"So…that Carolyn. A friend of yours?"

"Not really. Our husbands worked together, and we all belonged to the golf club."

"Ah," he said. "Hence her getup."

She thought of Carolyn in her coordinating I'm-a-golfer ensemble. She liked Henry's smirky mouth as he commented on it.

"Are you going?"

She looked at him questioningly.

"To the soiree at the country club. When I walked in, she was stressing how important it is that you attend as a new store owner."

"As I recall, she really hopes you'll be there. You know, based on the business card she slipped you."

Their lunches were delivered, and for a moment each indulged in enjoying their warm soup.

"So?" she asked.

"I don't know. Like I said, it all depends. How about you?"

She made a face.

"You're going to skip it?"

"I shouldn't, but I'd like to."

"Not your scene, huh?"

She met his gaze. "It never was even when William was alive."

"What is your scene?"

"Me?" She laughed softly. "I'd rather be in my jeans and sweatshirt taking a walk along the river."

"You're not avoiding going to this thing because you think I might show up, are you?"

"No." She scoffed. "Of course not."

"I know I make you jumpy."

She raised her chin to him. "You do not make me jumpy." She ladled soup to her lips.

"I'm just saying if having me around disturbs you and I go to the event, I could just steer clear of you."

She held his gaze. He was daring her. Despite the heat that bathed her face, she straightened her shoulders. Even if he was a golden god, she was not afraid to be in his company at a dinner dance.

"Whether you're planning to attend or not certainly does not factor in my decision."

That unnervingly attractive half smile landed on his mouth again. She held his gaze despite the smile.

"Good." He bit off the tip of his gooey cheese sandwich.

"Good."

"So it could be that we both show up," Henry said with a shrug.

"I guess it could happen."

He leaned in closer. "Hope they have margaritas."

She shook her head. "Eat your soup, man."

Chapter Eleven

Sid was resting in his room when Henry got there.

Navigating the tile floor, he crept as soundlessly as he could in his boots. He sat in the guest chair, feeling antsy. Just knowing he had to wait for the doctor to speak with him made it worse.

Being alone in a room with Sid had never been a comfort zone for him. They had always rubbed each other the wrong way, and time and distance hadn't changed that one bit.

The old man's eyes fluttered open, and he studied Henry as if he were a species he'd never seen before.

"Hello, Sid," Henry said.

Sid didn't answer. Henry scanned the old guy's face, and he seemed older and frailer than he had yesterday. Yet energy in his dark eyes bored into him.

"Can I get you something?"

Sid's tongue darted out and ran over his lips.

"You thirsty, Sid?"

"I could use some water."

Henry grabbed the cup sitting on the bedside table and poured water from a plastic pitcher. He extended it to Sid, who did not move to take it.

"Arm's not working right. Just leave it." Sid clicked his tongue in annoyance. "The nurse will help me." His voice was froggy but strong.

Henry pushed up from the chair and took a step

closer to the man in the bed. Sid's lips were cracked and dry. "You better drink." He lifted the cup.

"You can't help me." He clucked his tongue again.

Henry was about to return the cup to the table when his gaze caught the cellophane-wrapped straw lying on the surface. He removed it from its covering and jabbed it into the cup of water. He put the cup up close to Sid's face, the awkwardness of the gesture overridden by the zip of daring pounding in his chest.

"What are you doing?" The old man scrunched up his face, a myriad of wrinkles deepening in his sallow skin.

The rush of daring propelling him, Henry nudged the straw to Sid's lips. "Just drink it, Sid."

"Cripes, you putz."

"Take a sip." He pushed harder, errantly enjoying how the end of the straw poked at Sid's mouth. He gave it another push. Poke, poke, poke.

"Get that out of my face."

"Not until you drink."

They stared each other down, their long, steady gazes locked in defiance. Finally, Sid feebly opened his mouth, his lips quivering as they parted, eager like a baby bird waiting for a worm. The old man locked his parched lips around the straw, the crevices surrounding his mouth deep and dry, and sucked in. Some of the water dribbled down the saggy left side of his mouth, but enough of the liquid went down to quench his thirst. The sight sobered Henry.

Doctor Marshall came into the room with a greeting of "Hello, gentlemen."

Henry put the water cup down on the table and waited. He and the doctor shook hands.

"I'm glad to get the chance to tell you what a pleasure it is to meet the Hawk."

Henry ignored Sid's distinct harrumph. "Long time ago."

The doctor shook his head. "Not so very long, but boy, back in the day you sure had an arm."

He took a deep breath of medicinal air. "So how's Sid doing?"

"Give us a few minutes, then you and I can talk, okay?"

"Okay, I'll wait out in the hallway."

The doctor emerged from the room a few minutes later and spoke with assertive kindness as his words penetrated Henry's brain. All Henry could do was nod at what the man said. Even while the doctor said goodbye, Henry still felt numb. He watched the doctor make his way down the corridor, his footfalls squeaky on the shiny tile floor. As he trod along his path, the good doctor patted an orderly on his back and paused to say hello to visitors standing outside another patient's doorway. No one would know the man had just sent Henry's world on full tilt.

Henry was still trying to wrap his brain around Sid's medical situation. The stroke had impaired the use of his left side. He had limited movement in both his arm and leg. The palsy in his face was evident, though the doctor was sure it would eventually get better. But the limbs would need rehabilitation along with the hip. That was going to require first some PT sessions at a rehab facility, and eventually he would be well enough to continue sessions as an outpatient. When Henry's question came, in the calmest voice he could muster, about the time frame of all Sid's care, the doctor could not give him any specifics. His answer had been "wait and see." Henry didn't have it in him to wait, and how was he supposed to see if he was back in his apartment in New York? He blocked out the doctor's comment about his being unsure if Sid could ever live alone again. What the hell was he supposed to do about that?

For now, Sid was staying in the hospital until his team was sure he was strong enough for physical therapy and that there were no small strokes on his horizon. They called those events *transient ischemic attacks*, assaults that mimicked the aftershocks of an earthquake.

The doctor's words rattled Henry just like those aftershocks he spoke of. What this all meant for Henry was that he wasn't going home anytime soon.

Back in Sid's room, the old guy's eyes were closed, and his chest lifted and fell with the intake of shallow breaths. Henry didn't want to wake him from his nap and was selfishly glad he didn't have to discuss the doctor's findings with him.

Right now, he just didn't have words, and he momentarily wished he'd stayed the hell in New York in the first place. He wondered what would have happened to Sid if Henry didn't exist. Certainly, the old coot would receive proper care. He filled his lungs and let the air escape in a whoosh. *What ifs* made no sense. He'd done that plenty of times since his night on the steep, snowy ski slope, and it had done him no damn good.

His eyes did a sweep over the deathly still body tucked under the sheet. Sid had nobody else on this planet who could assist him with what lay ahead, and that truth was what kept Henry right here in Sycamore

River.

He quietly left the room and made his way through the hospital with one thing certain in his head. He'd have to make a stop again to the liquor store. He was going to need more beer.

Chapter Twelve

Megan arranged a bookcase with used paperbacks and hardcovers that had been donated to her store by people who hosted a street-wide garage sale a couple of weeks back.

She ran an appreciative hand over the covers, recognizing those books she'd read, her favorite, *Little Women*, and the compelling *To Kill a Mockingbird*. She decided to charge just a dollar for the hardbound volumes and half that for the paperbacks. Anyone that wanted a book should have a book.

Her store was shaping up, and she couldn't wait to be officially part of the community's quaint downtown. The thought brought to mind the upcoming gala at the country club. Lucy had been adamant that Megan should attend the event, and she'd been just as sure that she could skip it. Now, though, as the event approached and her store was nearing readiness, she saw the benefit of being there, of representing the Hope Chest as part of Sycamore River's downtown. And the possible appearance of Henry Denhawk was just something she'd have to deal with.

The vintage tablecloths she'd purchased from a house sale were washed and ready for ironing. She set up an ironing board right in the shop and began the task of making the table coverings smooth and crisp.

Ticking off a good number of items on the day's

to-do list was satisfying. After lunch she'd taken her vehicle in for servicing to the car dealership. She'd noticed a kind of sputtering sound when she accelerated and wasn't taking any chances. Plus, this was the second time her dashboard had flashed the "check engine" light. Last time the mechanic she'd gone to couldn't find anything wrong. She didn't feel comfortable riding around with a warning flashing in her face.

Lucy breezed in through the door. "Get your coat," she said in her typical brand of drama.

"I have to iron."

"You're going to want to join me."

Megan put the iron down on its end. "I know I'm going to regret asking this, but what are you talking about?"

"If your fairy godmother were to suddenly appear and wave her wand to produce your ideal house, what would it be?"

"You know what it would be."

"Say it."

"A small cottage on the river." She couldn't help it; her heart whirred in her chest.

The number of smaller homes in Sycamore River was diminishing due to the gentrification of the town. New subdivisions were showing up in the far reaches of town that used to be farms, and the houses on the river were what Lucy called "prime real estate." Some of the older houses on River Road had been knocked down, and big modern two-stories were built now instead. Megan loved the cottages with their charm as they dotted the landscape along the riverbank.

Lucy teasingly dangled a key. "There's a sweet

little fixer-upper on River Road that's going up on the market in a day or so. The office wants me to go preview it, and I thought you'd like to come along."

"Hell yeah, I would." Megan turned off the iron and went to grab her coat and purse.

****

The cottage at Two River Road had a weathered look with its natural cedar shakes aged to a silvery gray. The wine-colored front door was a sharp, pleasing contrast. A neglected flowerbed was ringed by fieldstone. Megan's heart swelled. This was love at first sight.

She and Lucy went up the three front steps, in dire need of paint, and Megan took in the front porch. She could just picture pots of geraniums and a wicker settee.

"Ready?" Lucy flashed her a look, her eyes lit with anticipation.

"I might burst."

Chuckling, Lucy inserted the key, and they went in. The place was small, cozy, and inviting. A fieldstone fireplace flanked the far wall of the living room, and the floorboards were honeyed with age.

The sunny kitchen was vintage with white-painted cabinets and a wooden floor. French doors led to a rather rickety-looking deck, and the backyard needed a sickle.

There were two bedrooms and two baths, one with a claw-foot tub. Megan turned to Lucy.

"I'm in love."

"Cute, right?"

"Oh, Lucy, most of my money's tied up with the Hope Chest. There's no way I could swing this now."

"Timing," Lucy lamented.

Megan walked the rooms again and actually felt the pull of belonging that made no sense. She'd been in the space for all of five or ten minutes, but a feeling of kinship came to her real as real.

They went outside and walked around the overgrown lawn bestrewn with raggedy-looking trees that needed a good pruning. She remembered how meticulous William was with his lawn, always out there fussing about with his clippers and such. If William were alive, he'd take a look at this place and laugh. But Megan saw beyond the neglect. She saw the potential for her heart's desire.

They got into Lucy's late-model compact, drove up the driveway, and turned onto River Road. They snaked their way around the bend and turned onto South Belair Drive.

"Where are we going?"

"Just making sure the Laurence house is still for sale by owner. We're hoping they give our office the listing. Stella, my manager, says they're close."

Megan knew the Laurence house. The large colonial was lovely as it sat regally on the grassy knoll of the well-kept lawn artfully decorated with multicolored fallen leaves. The house commanded admiration for its classic elegance. The place reminded her of the home she and William shared. It, too, had that wow factor with its gabled roof and grand front porch.

Lucy peered out the side window. "Yup. Still looking to sell on their own."

Megan spotted the sign for a house sale scheduled for yesterday and today. Her heart quickened. "Oh man, they're doing an estate sale. What a time for me not to have my SUV."

"I have an appointment scheduled in a few minutes, Megs, but I could spare a little bit of time if you want us to go in and peruse."

"No, that's okay. Besides, I like to go to these kinds of sales at the eleventh hour when all the expensive stuff and the antiques are gone. I get a lot of bargains when I show up late."

Many times, she'd get lucky purchasing odd pieces that no one looking for a treasure wanted. What those folks didn't know was that people who frequented thrift shops found treasures in the everyday things, the utilitarian items many people just picked up at a department store or ordered online without a blink of their eyes. Without a vehicle, she'd miss out on this one, and it pissed her off.

"You sure? I mean, as you can see, I can't fit much of anything in this little buggy of mine. But I'm game to go take a look if you want to."

"Thanks anyway, Lucy. I guess I'll just have to skip this one."

Lucy dropped her off at the Hope Chest and went on her way to her meeting with a potential client. Megan thought about the sale at the Laurence house and regretted having to miss it. But she was still basking in the memory of the little cottage on River Road. What a honey of a house. She was missing out on that, too.

She resumed her task of ironing the tablecloths and enjoyed the process of making wrinkly things smooth. The cloth she pulled from the bunch was decorated with rosy-red strawberries cross-stitched around the edges. She ran the heavy iron over the sturdy duck cloth, and steam billowed up and over the fabric. The task satisfied her and helped quell her disappointment about the estate sale at the Laurence house and the poor timing of that little cottage about to come on the market. She just hoped someone didn't come along and buy it for the land and plow the cute house down to a pile of rubble.

A little while later Henry walked into her store, that slash of a smile on his luscious mouth. Lord, she had never had this kind of sexual electricity with someone. A pang of guilt hit her hard. She'd never voice the words, but in truth she and William hadn't had this kind of raw sexual attraction. She'd loved William, of course, but what she felt when she was in Henry's proximity was something out of this world. But the reality of the situation kept her from doing anything but reminisce about the night they'd spent together. There was no sense in acting on impulse, not with a guy ready to leave town as fast as he could. Timing's cruelty was doing a number on her today.

"You never stop, huh?" Henry came closer.

She did her best to concentrate on her task. "You've got to make hay when the sun shines, I guess."

"What's all this?"

The lines by his mouth seemed more defined today. She wondered if the weight of his circumstances was getting to him. This wasn't the guy she'd hooked up with. That Henry had been free and easy, appealing in her multiple-margarita stupor. So much for keeping those memories at bay. She flipped the tablecloth to run the steamy iron on the other side.

"I bought a bunch of old tablecloths at a house sale. I laundered them, and now I'm making them pretty."

He touched one of the cloths that hung folded over the bar of a coat hanger. "People like this stuff, huh?"

"Yes." Why was she so defensive? Everything he said didn't have to be a knock. Maybe he just had no clue what some people would want from a thrift store. She willed herself to chill out. "You'd be surprised."

"I wasn't sure you'd be here."

She smiled as she worked. "I practically live here."

"I didn't see your vehicle."

"Yeah." She made a face. "It's in the shop. Hopefully, I'll have it back in a day or so. How's Sid?"

"He's in his room, awake, and they're getting him strong enough to eventually move to a rehab facility." He shook his head. "Sid's going to need a lot of rehab, a lot of attention." Cloudiness moved into his sky-blue eyes.

"What's that mean for you?" She hung the freshly ironed fabric on a hanger and hooked it on the stainless-steel rack. She grabbed another tablecloth and smoothed it on the surface of the ironing board.

He shrugged. "It's tricky. But I'll figure it out. I might run out and get some more cat food for Mookie. Can I get you anything?"

An idea came to her, and her mind debated it. She let her gaze flit over him as she mustered up the nerve.

"Are you going to the store now?" Her question was casual. At least she hoped that's how it sounded.

"I've got a phone call to make to my agent, then I was going to head over to the Acme. Besides the cat food, I thought I'd stock up a little on some groceries for myself since I'm going to be here longer than I thought. I'd be glad to pick up anything you might need."

"Well, there is something I could use, but it's a lot to ask."

"Try me."

"Okay. I frequent estate sales after the expensive items are already gone. I often get major bargains at these sales when they are about to close down for the day. There's a sale here in town today and"—she checked her fitness tracker—"right about now they're down to the wire."

He locked his gaze onto hers, and she stood there with her breath captive in her chest. Her mind kept screaming at her with "What are you doing?" but she ignored it.

"Let's do it."

"Yeah?" She couldn't help it. She was glad, almost giddy with anticipation. She turned off the iron. "Really?"

"Sure."

"Great. Let me go freshen up a bit and grab my purse. I'll be right back."

****

Henry was examining the hope chest when she came back into the room.

"So I'm assuming this cabinet's your store's namesake?" His hand gently moved across the surface.

"It is."

"You keep it locked?"

She cleared her throat. "Unfortunately, I, uh, lost the key."

"That's too bad."

"The day we were in the cemetery."

"What?"

"I had the key in the pocket of my sweater, and

then after the, you know, chase with the dog, it must have dropped out."

"Oh no, really? Did you go back and see if the key was in the grass anywhere?"

"Yes, but the grounds crew was there mowing the lawns and blowing leaves. God only knows where that key went."

"Well, that stinks. Can you get a locksmith in here to duplicate a key? I'd be happy to pay for it."

"Thank you for that, and yes, I suppose I can, but there's something about losing the original that makes me sad. Besides, right now I'm concentrating on getting the store open on October thirty-first."

"That's soon. Will it be ready?" he asked.

"Yes."

For the first time she was truly confident. The Hope Chest would be ready for business.

He opened the door for her, and she locked the store. She hopped into the passenger side of his truck, and he went around and got in on the driver's side. He started the engine. She couldn't believe she was here in his truck, sitting beside him. The interior of the truck was neat, the leather seats rich looking. A pine scent came from an air freshener dangling from the rearview mirror. This was no big deal, but her blood rushed through her veins as if it couldn't wait to go for a ride.

"Where to, milady?"

Did he practice that charm, or did it just ooze out of him like sap from a tree? It didn't matter if he was pouring it on. She liked it. Her body vibrated, was jazzed for being here with him in this enclosed space. She felt daring, a bit like the night she'd met him at the bar in the city.

"We're going to South Belair Drive."

"Okay, I know just where that is."

"It's just off River Road," she added.

He nodded, and they fell silent as he made his way through the winding roadway. She tried to keep her eyes forward, but the betraying orbs liked stealing glances of him while he concentrated on the road.

"I'm really sorry about the key to your cabinet."

"I appreciate that, thank you. But it's my fault for sticking the key in my pocket."

"Why do they call it a hope chest, by the way?"

She chuckled. "You've never heard of a hope chest?"

"No."

"The practice goes back more than a hundred years. When a young woman became the age of having a male suiter ask for her hand, she was given a hope chest by her mother or some other female relative. The chest was for storing items she'd save for when she got married, when she made her own life."

"You mean like pots and pans and stuff?"

She laughed aloud. "Yeah, women were dying to have pots and pans. No. Delicate things, meaningful things, heirlooms and mementos, things like that. You know, things like an embroidered tablecloth her grandmother made for her or doilies she made herself, maybe a crocheted hankie from her mom, a pretty brush-and-comb set from her groom-to-be. Sentimental things."

"You're a romantic."

Heat climbed her face. "Something wrong with that?"

He flashed her a look, then turned his attention

back to his driving. "Not at all. It's just that I didn't see that side of you on the night we met."

"We're not discussing the night we met."

He chuckled. "But you can't say you haven't thought about it."

"Just pay attention to the road, okay?"

He smiled as he drove. "So now I know what a hope chest is. They don't do that kind of stuff nowadays, though, huh?"

"No, not in that sense, but in another sense we all do."

He glanced at her. "How so?"

"Everyone has hopes and dreams for something, anticipation for what we want. In that way we collect precious items for that eventuality. Like, when I knew it was time for me to really take the idea of opening a thrift shop seriously, I started collecting, in a way. Searched available storefronts, went to garage sales for items I thought would be good. Things like that."

"I get it. The hope chest served as kind of a wish list."

"Yes. Nowadays people make vision boards." She laughed. "You've heard of those, I assume."

"I think so."

She shook her head.

"Listen, let me say something. I know I've apologized already, but I really am sorry for that day in the cemetery and most of all for not immediately recognizing you. It took me a second to register. I mean, who'd have expected that we'd meet again in a graveyard of all places? What I'm trying to say is that you are not at all forgettable." He paused, then added, "Wild Irish rose."

Heat flooded her face, and she knew her Irish skin was turning a telltale pink. "Let me just say this about that night in the city." She stared straight ahead, breathing in, then out. *Just get it over with. Just say it, and it will be forgotten.*

"Okay." His tone of that one word was sultry, and she was already sorry she'd brought this up. But she wouldn't back down now.

"I never do anything like that. Have never picked up a guy in a bar. I thought I'd never see you again. I guess fate's been getting a good laugh on my account."

"Hey, the night we met, I knew immediately that you were treading on new turf."

"You did?"

He just nodded.

"How?" *Stop asking questions.*

He was about to respond when she noticed they had made it to Cedar Road. "Turn right here," she said.

The mood was lost, and she was just as glad. She needed to learn to keep her thoughts to herself and her big mouth shut.

The Laurence house came into view.

"I remember this place from when I was a kid. Nice," Henry said as he parked his truck along the curb in front of the house.

Cars lined up along the street as well, and a couple emerged from the house carrying a large oil painting, a landscape scene.

Megan eyed the place again. "William's and my house was similar. Ours wasn't as big, though."

He studied her for a moment. "And you don't own it anymore?"

She shook her head. "No. I sold it after William

passed. The proceeds allowed me to venture into opening my store. But eventually I'd like to buy another house. For now, I'm staying with my friend Lucy."

"Do you miss the house you had?"

"The truth? I never really felt at home there. Don't get me wrong. It was beautiful, but to me, it was like when you try on an article of clothing and you know that it's just not you. It itches you, makes you uncomfortable."

He nodded as if he understood. "So what are you looking for when you do buy?"

She gazed out the windshield. People were still entering and leaving the Laurence house. "We should wait a few minutes until the crowd thins before going in." She turned to him. "You okay with that?"

"Sure, but how come?"

"The items I'm looking to snag are the ones that are left behind. And price-wise it's best when the owner thinks I'm their last hope to unload what's left."

A smile broke out across his mouth. "Business strategy. I get it." He leaned back in his seat and tilted his head. "Okay, let's see. What were we talking about?"

She was not going to let him elaborate on how he knew she was a novice in the art of pickups.

"Houses." She looked out the passenger window and zeroed in on the roadway that curved around toward River Road. "Want to walk for a little bit? I'll show you the kind of house I like."

He turned off the ignition and put his key fob into the pocket of his jacket. "Lead the way."

They strode down to River Road and made their way along the houses overlooking the river. It was an eclectic neighborhood, different from the more traditional homes on South Belair. No two houses were the same on River Road. A bungalow could be next door to a three-story modern edifice, and no one would blink an eye. Most of the houses were small, though, and all of them had decks or porches that took advantage of the river beyond their properties. This was her hope. A house on the river.

"I'm getting the idea of what makes you tick," Henry said as he eyed the neighborhood. "You're not a Georgian-colonial type. You're Craftsman."

She laughed. "I'm so Craftsman."

"Did you grow up in a Craftsman-type house?"

She couldn't hold back the scoffing sound of her laugh. "Not by a long shot. I was raised by an aunt, and we lived in a small row house in a Chicago suburb."

"Ah, so you're eager to find yourself a Craftsman to call your own."

She flashed him a smile.

They walked on until the dead end where the parkland began. "See this one? It's about to go on the market. Lucy previewed it and brought me along."

She watched as Henry scanned the cottage at Two River Road. She took in the charm that some people might think was chic-free shabby. The eucalyptus wreath that hung on the front door was cockeyed. A weed grew tall and spindly out of a flowerpot on the top step.

"It just needs some TLC. Actually, when I first saw this house, I was feeling a little like Natalie Wood in *Miracle on Thirty-Fourth Street*."

He grinned. "Not sure what that means, but I'm guessing you like the place."

"You don't know the old movie?"

"I do like old movies, but Cagney and Garfield types. I like gangsters."

"Well, in *Miracle on Thirty-Fourth Street*, a little girl asks Santa for a house for her family, and she spots it from her parents' car as they are driving down a street. It's magical."

"Hmmmm. Unless Santa has started to work in real estate in his off-season, I'm going to guess he's not about to give out a magic house."

She couldn't help it; she laughed. His likability was dangerous. She was so much better off when she thought he was a stranger she'd never see again.

"Maybe not, but this is just what I'd wish for." She did a little jump. "It's empty. Want to look in the windows?"

She didn't wait for his response and bolted up the stairs and onto the porch. She cupped her hands by her eyes as she peered in a front window. "I just love that fieldstone fireplace. Look."

Henry leaned in close, close enough that she could smell his appealing pine-scented aftershave.

"That is nice. In good condition, too."

"And guess what? The master bathroom has a cast-iron claw-foot tub. It's huge. We could both fit in it." Her face flushed hot the moment the words escaped her mouth. The picture she painted parked itself in her head and taunted her.

Henry laughed. "Good to know."

When they got to the back of the house, he went up on the deck and scrutinized it. "Might need a whole new deck. The boards are uneven, and they're bowed. See?" He bent down and ran a hand along a dip in a board. "This must puddle like crazy after a rain."

"You sound like a man in the know."

"These last four years I've been doing some carpentry with a buddy of mine's crew."

"So with your expert eye, would you say this cottage could be a money pit?"

"Not at all. But don't get me wrong. It's going to need work. I like it, though. And the view of the river from the deck is priceless."

They shared a glance. "Yes," she said in a near whisper.

****

They made their way back, and as they rounded the corner, the Laurence house came into view. Fewer cars were parked at the curb. The time was right.

"Okay, let's do this," she said.

Together they strode up the brick walkway while her mind pelted her with questions. How had this happened? How did she and the hookup guy become friends of a sort? She would never have guessed in a million years that this guy would be in her orbit, let alone even seeing his face again after that night in the city. Life was full of surprises. Henry pressed the doorbell, and they waited.

The front door opened, and a tall man in a deep-blue crewneck sweater greeted them with a motion of his hand. "You're in under the wire."

"We're not too late, are we?" Megan knew he'd never tell them yes. She'd done this before.

"No, no." The man waved his hand again. "Take your time."

The foyer was a large rectangle, the floor a deep, aged wood. A grandfather clock sat prominently against one wall. From it dangled a tag that boasted "Sold."

They moved through the rooms, the living room, the dining room, a study, the kitchen. Pieces of furniture and collectibles were on display, everything bearing a price tag. A melancholy sadness came over Megan. Was there no one in the lineage of the Laurence clan who would have wanted any of these items that remained here after the picking? She touched items on display, ceramic flowerpots, glass vases, bric-a-brac, searching for those things that "spoke" to her. She would buy those things and sell them at the Hope Chest, where they'd be given a new life.

"See anything that catches your eye?"

Momentarily she had forgotten Henry Denhawk was at her side. "Yes, I don't know where to begin."

"Maybe we're better off looking at everything and then going back and picking out what you really want."

At that moment a man and woman claimed a highboy, and a red "Sold" sticker was applied to it.

"I don't think there's too much time to mull what to get. I think I need to see what speaks to me."

She ignored the smirk on his mouth, considering that he was helping her.

They came upon a shiny black baby grand piano in the living room where a tent card prominently announced "Not for Sale." On top of the piano, a white intricately crocheted scarf resembling an old Irish shawl draped artfully. She moved closer to get a better look. Henry followed.

On top of the scarf, a series of silver picture frames was displayed, some bigger, some smaller, some made of decorative filigree, others smooth and shiny, but all of them silver. In each frame was a black-and-white photograph of someone presumably from the Laurence family. A young girl with her bicycle smiled broadly for the camera. A photo of an older couple, the man dapper in a dark suit, the woman classic in a well-fitted skirt and blouse. She glanced at the group photos and several portrait photos, and they mesmerized her.

"Makes you wonder where all these people are now, huh?" Henry asked.

"Yes. Certainly, there has to be someone left in this family who would want these treasures."

He nodded at her comment as they walked away from the piano.

In less than an hour, she had laid claim to a very nice porcelain tea service, white with tiny hand-painted pink flowers scattered over the pieces, an oak dresser with nice brass hardware, a small writing desk, and an old record player in a wooden case. The tag on the player had said that it was sold "as is," which told her the device probably didn't work, but she just loved the hand-carved cabinet, and the price was ridiculously low. Hopefully, someone would come into her store and fall in love with it.

She had to admit that Henry did most of the work. He borrowed the company in charge's hand truck, wrapped the pieces in old sheets she had brought with her, and stored the items in a tight arrangement in the back of his vehicle.

When they were settled in the truck and ready to go, she turned to him. "Thank you again, Henry, for agreeing to come with me."

Before he could respond, a knock sounded on his driver's side window. A man with a full head of short-cropped steel-gray hair stood outside the glass.

Henry rolled down the pane. "Coach!" He stuck his hand out of the open window and shook hands with the man.

"What do you know?" the man said, his face bright and happy. "I don't see you for years, and now I'm always running into you. I must be lucky."

"What are you doing here?"

"Just being nosey, seeing what's doing. My wife lives for house sales. I see you two had some finds." He leaned in and caught Megan's eye. "Hi, there. I'm Lou Brennen. This guy was my star ballplayer back when he was a kid."

"Hello," she said. "I'm Megan Harris. Henry was kind enough to help me pick up some things for the thrift shop I'm opening downtown."

"Oh." Lou clapped Henry on the shoulder. "A Good Samaritan, huh? 'Bout time." He chuckled. "You finally turning that new leaf?"

Henry quipped, "You're still a comedian."

"Hey, thanks again for stopping by to meet the team. The kids are still talking about it. I hope you can come see us again soon. The boys would enjoy it."

"How's the new coach doing?"

Lou made a face. "Good guy and everything, but he's going to need to toughen up like I told you. These kids will walk all over him if he doesn't. If you remember, I didn't take any nonsense. Especially from you." He laughed again. He leaned in and directed his attention to Megan. "This one was a trip. Best athlete I ever coached, to tell you the truth, but what a pill."

She chuckled. Henry's former coach seemed like a good guy. She liked him.

"How's Sid?"

"He's coming along, Coach. They're waiting for him to be strong enough to transfer to a rehab center."

Lou nodded. "Hope it all works out for the guy."

"Thanks."

"Nice meeting you, Megan," he said as he stepped away from the truck. "And good luck with the thrift shop. Wait until I tell my wife. She'll be a constant customer." He pointed to Henry. "Don't be a stranger. We could use your expertise."

On the way back to her store, Megan studied Henry's profile. She tried to imagine him as a young boy under the tutelage of his former coach. No surprise that he'd been a "handful."

"He seemed nice," she said, looking to fill the space in the truck.

Henry appeared deep in thought. "He's a good guy. A really good guy."

"So you stopped in to see his team. That was nice."

He didn't respond, kept his eyes on the road.

"You think you'll go see them again, like he asked?"

"Nah. I won't have time for that. I've got an important meeting on Friday with the Mets organization about a job, and if that goes well, I'll be all tied up. Between that and Sid, you know?"

"Yes." She had no reason to feel one way or the other about his plans to be in New York for all or most of the time. She'd known that. Yet a ding of disappointment pinched inside her.

They drove the rest of the way in silence. She wondered about him, couldn't help it. She hadn't spent much time with him but had already decided he was anxious to detach from his past as though he were trying to outrun his own memories.

She understood that too well. Thinking of her life as William's wife could be comforting, sometimes not. Sometimes she'd get so lonely she'd want to weep. She did her best not to think too far back, back to the days when she was in Chicago, a skinny young girl working around the clock to make ends meet. The one bright spot from that time was the home she'd made for herself in that tiny apartment above the liquor store, a haven far and away from Aunt Gemma. She'd bought furniture and household items from a thrift store, and now she was providing the same service to others. That felt right. A niggle of something, happiness maybe, gave her a jolt like a sudden chill to her skin that evoked goose bumps.

She let her gaze flit over the man beside her, his golden hair askew from the breeze coming in from his open window. His hands on the wheel looked strong, and yet she knew his hands to be gentle, too. She closed her eyes, but she still saw him in her mind.

She wished he'd roll up that damn window. The breeze gave her such a chill.

Chapter Thirteen

Henry moved Megan's purchases into her store using the borrowed hand truck. He was surprised at how much he enjoyed the outing. The walk along River Road had been interesting, and he liked getting to understand the woman who intrigued him more and more. She was not a fan of the ostentatious. He'd have thought her romantic notions about old pieces of furniture and her preference to small cottages over stately colonials would have proved he and Megan had nothing in common. But that was not the case. Megan Harris was screwing with his head, and he didn't hate it.

He was glad to see Coach again, and he liked that the guy caught him helping Megan out with her purchases. For some reason he felt as if he were back in town for real and not just a visitor dying to return to New York. The feeling was fleeting, but he hadn't hated that either.

Lou's invitation for him to come watch the kids again hung in his mind. He probably wouldn't go, but he was tempted. Seeing those kids reminded him of when baseball was the sport he loved, the hope for his future. So many things had changed since those days.

"That should do it," he said. Megan stood there all but petting the items she purchased. She was a funny sort. The women he'd known wouldn't get excited about some old dresser unless maybe each drawer was filled with diamonds or clothing from a designer boutique. He didn't know how to react to a woman like Megan, this proud yet approachable person who wasn't afraid to show the world who she was.

"Thank you again." Her face was lit up as if she'd walked into a roomful of presents. She didn't see used furniture; she saw treasures.

A smile slid across his mouth. "So we're even, then?"

Questions flooded her honey-colored eyes. "Even?"

"You know, the whole thing at the cemetery."

"Ah. Okay, yes. We're even."

"Except for the locksmith. I intend to arrange for someone to come and make you a new key for your hope chest."

"Henry, really you don't have to do that. I can take care of it. Besides, I don't know for sure I lost the key at the cemetery. I could have washed it down the drain by accident."

"Still doing it."

She shook her head. "I'm starting to believe your former coach. You are a piece of work."

"So"—he ran a hand over the phonograph case—"you think this thing works?"

"I'll bet not." She laughed. "But somehow I had to have it."

"I know. It called to you." He opened the lid and delicately took the arm into his hands. He looked underneath and fiddled with something.

"You making fun of me?"

"Not at all," he said, but he couldn't hide his smirky grin. God, she was cute. "Look." He showed her a small metal item pinched between his thumb and forefinger. "The needle is broken. The tip is snapped off. You're going to need a new needle."

"That can't be easy to find."

"Not sure how readily available phonograph needles are these days, but there's a music store in town, isn't there?"

"Yes, down about a block and a half. Marty's Music."

"Tell you what," he said as he put the needle in his shirt pocket. "I'll stop into Marty's on my way back from the hospital."

"You don't have to do that."

"Seriously, it's not a problem."

"Well, thank you. I didn't even think about whether or not this thing was functioning. I just fell in love with the cabinet."

"When something calls, right? I think the pictures on the piano had that effect on you, too."

"They did. I can't stop thinking about them."

"It's kind of sad. To think all that living took place among all those people, and now maybe nobody's around to remember."

She tilted her head. "That's one way to look at it. But to me, it's a privilege of life to have those special moments that mean so much you want to capture them for all time. If you're the one that got to live those moments, you're the lucky one. Preserving them in a frame is just icing on the cake. Those photos are memories that life was well lived in that house."

He studied her. She was a good woman, and she had started to scare the ever-living hell out of him.

"I'm going to run the hand truck back to the

Laurence house and then swing by and check on Sid."

"Okay, thank you again for your help. I couldn't have done this without you."

He left before he convinced himself not to.

Chapter Fourteen

Since it was her turn to provide dinner, Megan went home with takeout from Romanelli's. They made the best eggplant parm, and she and Lucy loved it.

"I officially hired that college girl, Mandy. We arranged the hours she'll work at the store that won't interfere with her class schedule. Can you believe it? I have an employee."

Lucy proffered a tired-looking smile. "Look at you being all pleased with yourself. I like it."

While they enjoyed their meal, Lucy seemed quiet, introspective, which was so unusual for the normally upbeat, lighthearted woman.

"What's up, Lucy?"

"You can tell, huh?"

"You okay?"

"Oh, I'm fine, but I can't believe I did it again."

For Lucy, that could mean a myriad of things. Megan waited for her to continue.

"I trusted this guy who works for another realty firm. He and I had drinks and appetizers one night at Jabberwocky's. He's cute and funny and smart, and I was kind of into him."

"Sounds good so far. What happened, though?"

"Well, I slept with him. I'm not proud of it. I'm an idiot, but yeah, I went back to his place, and that's what happened. And the very next day he stole a listing right out from under me."

"Oh, Lucy, that's terrible."

"I can't believe I didn't see that he was full of crap. I mean, I'm not stupid. At least, I don't think I am."

"You're brilliant. Stop. It's not you. He's an ass."

"Yeah, but I should have seen signs."

Megan took a deep breath. She was too full to eat any more of her dinner. Normally she could polish off most of her meal, but tonight she couldn't take another bite.

She couldn't help but think of Henry while Lucy spoke of the louse of a guy she'd been involved with. She still found it hard to believe that she slept with a stranger and now that stranger had turned into a friend, if friends made your whole body tremble with just one slow, sexy smile. In truth, she looked forward to when he came home and had to use her store to get to Sid's apartment. So much for wishing the workmen out at the back porch would finish their job. Now she could not help but wonder if she was setting herself up the same way Lucy had.

"Lucy, I'd give you advice, but as you recall, I'm kind of the poster child for what not to do when it comes to men."

Lucy chuckled. "Thanks for making me laugh. I want a glass of wine. Join me?"

She wrinkled her nose. The idea of wine didn't appeal to her these days. "Just keep in mind that it's a good thing this jerk who swindled you out of a listing is out of your life. Let him have the damn listing. Who cares?"

Lucy opened the bottle of merlot and poured herself a measure into a wineglass. She took a sip. "You know how I was trying to talk you into the guy that owns the bookstore?"

"Yes, Mr. Topsoil."

Lucy grinned and shook her head. "Pete Moss."

"Of course," Megan said, glad she'd made her friend smile. "What about him?"

"The funniest thing. I went into his store looking for yet another self-help book. I swear I could build a house with all the self-help books I own. But that's what I do. Anyway, Peter and I had a conversation, and he's a nerd for sure, and his name is way odd, but I think he's the good kind of nerd. You know what I mean? And he's engaging and smart. You sure you're not interested in meeting him?"

"Hey, Luce, I was really just kidding about his name. I'm sure he's a straight-up kind of guy, and we know he likes books. That's a good thing, right? But I'm just not in the market to meet anyone."

Lucy took another sip of her wine. "Are you sure about that? I mean, you and the Hawk seem to be kind of cozy these days."

"He's leaving town. He can't wait to get back to his life in New York. There's nothing going on between us. Believe me."

Lucy drained the wine from her glass. "I'd like to fall in love. I'm going to be forty in two months. Two months! I'd like to get married and have a kid or two, you know? Find a good guy, be happy. You ever feel like the clock's ticking? Was I noticing the positives about Peter Moss because I'm man shopping? I'd hope not. That wouldn't be fair to him or me."

Megan took a deep breath and let it expel. "Can I tell you something, Lucy?"

"Anything."

"There are times when I can't help but think that's what happened with William and me. I mean, I wound up loving him, really loving him, but when I think about our relationship, I have to admit that what attracted me to William in the first place was his stability. Not very romantic." She took a long sip of her water. "I feel guilty about that."

"Stability can be very attractive. Bad boys haven't cornered the market on attractiveness."

She thought of Henry. Her physical reaction to the man was something she'd never experienced. But she was learning more about him, and the Hawk had more to him than those sky-blue eyes that could look right into her like an X-ray.

"I'm right behind you in turning forty." She pushed up from her chair and brought her plate to the sink and rinsed it. "I'd like to have a family, too. I was sure that my chance had died right along with William."

"And now?"

She bit down on her lip. What about now, indeed? She didn't know what the future held, but she'd come to know that she wanted everything. She wanted that stability and reliability, but she also wanted—no, needed—that heart-pounding, sappy demonstrative love she saw in the movies, the movies that usually starred Sandra Bullock.

She couldn't tell Lucy that now. It scared her too much just to think the thought. She changed tacks.

"I'm going back to the store for a while to get some more stuff done."

"Tonight?"

"Hey, Halloween is just about two weeks away.

That clock's really ticking."

Together they cleaned up the kitchen, and before Megan left, she pulled Lucy into an embrace.

"You are the sweetest person, Lucy. Don't let one stupid guy take away your light. So what if he got the listing. Hope it keeps him warm and cozy at night."

Lucy squeezed her back. "I love you."

"Back at you."

****

Megan tugged the zipper of her dress and was surprised the garment felt snug. She couldn't have gained weight. The Hope Chest had kept her running day and night. She pulled at the brick-red fabric of her favorite dress.

She slipped her feet into the black pumps and went to the kitchen to join Lucy, who was already waiting in her stunning navy-blue sheath.

"Yowzah," Lucy said when Megan strode into the room.

"Yowzah to you too, lady. Does my dress look too tight?"

"What? No way. It fits you perfectly. Totally accents your figure."

Megan peered down at the dress. Maybe she was just imagining the sense of confinement in the dress. After all, she spent most of her time these days in overalls or comfy old jeans.

On the ride over in Lucy's car, she wondered if Henry would be at the dinner tonight. He'd teased her when they were at the diner, had made a pretend bet that she wouldn't be able to resist a dance with him. Had that just been idle talk? Why did that matter? She chastised herself for having the man on her mind.

A valet opened the car door for them, and she and Lucy went into the lobby. The Sycamore River Country Club was just as she'd remembered it. Tasteful and understatedly upscale from the plush Persian rug to the multifaceted chandelier above their heads.

Cocktail hour was held in the pub where the large, dark-wooden bar was a busy place. Megan scanned the crowd, recognizing some of the faces from the days when she and William were club members. Carolyn Montgomery was at the bar with a gaggle of the ladies from their golf group. The group was laughing and looking jovial, and Megan was surprised that Carolyn did not seem in the thick of it. She stared into her martini instead, a faraway look in her eyes. The women with her didn't seem to notice as they bantered back and forth. Like the old days, a jab of unbelonging gave her a pinch. She averted her eyes, hoping none of them would see her there.

"I'm getting a drink. What can I get you?" Lucy asked.

"A seltzer."

"Come on, girl. Live it up a little. How about a cosmo?"

She shook her head. Her stomach was jittery, and she didn't want to ingest anything that might put her over the edge. She was here at this dinner as a representative of her new shop, and she needed to be at her best.

Waitstaff made their way through the throng with silver trays of shrimp toast triangles, pigs in blankets, stuffed mushroom caps, and the like. Megan accepted a tempura shrimp and nibbled while she watched the crowd.

Lucy joined her at a little round table near the wall. Elaine and Joe from the candy store stopped to say hello, as did Marty from the music store. He remembered that Henry had come in for the phonograph needle.

Peter Moss greeted them at their table. He looked nice, dapper even, in his gray suit, starchy shirt, and paisley tie. "You ladies look lovely," he offered. He raised his drink, a squat glass of clear liquid on ice.

"You don't look so bad yourself, Peter." Lucy touched her glass to his.

Megan wished she had that natural ability to be light and breezy with a member of the opposite sex. Except for her tequila-induced night in New York. God, would that memory ever leave her alone?

As if on cue, Henry Denhawk entered the room. Everyone around seemed to stop what they were doing just to get a look at him. Megan's heart acted as if it had been tossed into a washing machine stuck on the spin cycle. His dark blue suit had to be custom. The way it fit him just accentuated the man's solid, healthy body like a work of art. His hair was combed back over his crown, giving him a sophisticated look that showed off the God-given contours of his face. Lord Almighty, the man made quite the appearance.

Lucy smirked. "Oh, honey. You should see yourself."

"Stop."

She laughed. "Put your tongue back in your mouth."

"Oh my God, Lucy, be quiet. He's walking this way."

****

He saw her at a table in the corner. She had decided to attend after all. Something inside him squeezed. He was playing with fire, and he knew it. Megan Harris was not the sort to jump into a fling, although their first meeting might have indicated otherwise.

He adjusted his tie. Luckily, he'd picked up this suit for his meeting with the Mets, so he had it ready for the event at the country club.

"You got your dancing shoes on?" Cliff slipped up to his side, checking up on him. Always.

He pointed to his freshly polished wing tips.

"Hank, you surprise me. I didn't have to threaten bodily harm to get you to agree to show your face tonight. I'm speechless."

"You don't sound speechless." He searched the crowd again for Megan from his vantage point near the wall. She continued to smile and talk with the people at her table. He enjoyed getting to know her better. She was one of those people who was either in or out in any relationship and nothing in between. He'd been the king of in-between for four years, and it had served him like a spray coating that kept things from sticking.

"Seriously, I'm glad you realize the importance of this event to your career. I've got a photographer ready to sneak in and take some candids. Be sure to look engaged," Cliff said, pulling him away from thoughts of Megan.

"Jeez, Cliff, could you cool it with the pictures?"

"Leave that aspect to me. You just enjoy the ball, Cinderella."

"That's great advice." He snaked through the crowd, pausing to nod polite hellos to those who offered greetings, but he had one destination.

He approached her table, knowing he was walking right into smoldering embers, that time when a fire extinguished or ignited. When he caught her sweet-tea gaze that shone bright with welcome, Megan had become the bellows, and it did not stop him.

"Good evening," he said, his gaze solely on Megan. She looked different tonight in a form-fitting dress. A glimpse of cleavage at the neck reminded him of her skin's softness when he'd touched her there. A low twinge teased him.

She introduced him to the man with them, a guy named Peter who owned a local bookshop. Peter and Megan's friend, Lucy, seemed to be engaged in some lighthearted ribbing, and while they flirted, he and Megan were silently locked in an unrelenting stare. Finally, she cast her gaze down to her beverage. She lifted her hand, gently grasped the plastic straw, and began to stir the clear liquid around and around. He caught a glimpse of her shamrock tattoo, and the ache inside him gripped harder.

A waiter announced it was time for all to enter the ballroom, and slowly the crowd made its way through the open double doors.

Megan stood, and he followed her. He placed a daring hand at the small of her back with the excuse of maneuvering her through the bottleneck. He just wanted to touch her. She turned to meet his gaze, a smirk on her lips that told him she was on to him.

"You look amazing," he whispered.

"Thank you."

When he learned that he'd been seated at a table of local dignitaries, he was disappointed. He'd hoped to be at her table. The need to be near her spooked and enticed him all at the same time. The fact that she sat across the room on the other side of the dance floor only intensified the feeling.

Through their meal he engaged in nonsensical small talk with those at his table, and he periodically sought Megan's gaze. Whenever she lifted her eyes to greet his, it felt like a tiny victory of some kind.

Waitstaff began to clear dishes after the main course, and Henry took the opportunity to excuse himself from the table and meandered over to where Megan sat.

"Can I talk with you a moment?" He put his hand on the back of her chair.

She placed her linen napkin onto the table and stood. She directed her attention to Lucy. "I'll be right back."

They strode out of the dining room and back to the lounge area, where a few people had settled themselves around the bar.

"Can I get you something to drink?" He leaned up on the bar.

"I'm fine."

He ordered himself a scotch on the rocks. "Are you enjoying the night?" he asked as casually as he could muster. The look on her face told him she was wondering why he'd felt the need to bring her into this room, certainly not to ask whether she was having a good time.

"I have a confession," he said, not stopping to think before he spoke. He took a pull of his drink.

"Oh?" She scooted herself up onto a barstool. "I'd better sit for this." After she adjusted herself, one shapely leg crossing over the other, she locked on to his gaze. "Shoot."

He put his drink down on the bar and stood closer to her. He could smell her honeysuckle scent. "I'm only here tonight to see you. I'd have otherwise politely declined. So if the speeches are boring, I will most definitely blame you."

A grin broke out on her lips. "I'll take that under advisement."

"To make it up to me, you could dance with me once the music starts."

She shot him a skeptical look.

"Unless that worries you."

She snickered. "Worries me?"

"You know, being in such close proximity to me. Could be tempting."

"I think I can resist any wayward urges."

He lifted his glass and took another sip. "Good."

Her lips parted in mock protest, but he could tell she enjoyed the lighthearted flirting. When her face was lit up this way, she was irresistible, more appealing than any woman he'd ever known. He'd been joking, but maybe he was the one who should be worried.

****

Megan couldn't help the giddiness that ran through her. She knew damn well that Henry Denhawk had perfected the art of charm and that their conversation was surely pure malarkey, but she enjoyed it and ate it up like pablum.

So she'd agreed to a dance with him, and she secretly thought how he wouldn't have had to all but trick her into agreement. Tonight, even sans any tequila, she would be glad to step into his arms on the dance floor. The voice of reason, the tidbits of caution that knocked on her brain, could just sit it out. She was dancing.

Carolyn Montgomery burst into the lounge, her purse clutched in her hand and her coat slung over her arm. She made a beeline across the room toward them.

"Hi." She sounded breathy with concern.

"Everything okay, Carolyn?" Megan said.

"No, everything is not okay. Henry, I didn't want to bother you this evening, but I'm heading home now, and this is my only chance to speak with you before I go."

How can Carolyn be leaving? Isn't she running this shindig?

"Sure," Henry said. "What's on your mind?"

"It's about Joshua, my son. You remember—he's one of the pitchers for the high school team."

"Yes, of course. I know Joshua."

"He broke his wrist." Tears came to her eyes, and for the first time ever, Megan saw signs of age in Carolyn's otherwise perfect face. Crow's feet fanned at the corners of her eyes, and creases appeared beside her mouth. "He was skateboarding, which he knew not to do, but he fell and broke the wrist in two places."

"I'm sorry to hear that," Henry said.

"He's not going to be able to start when baseball season gets underway, and he's a junior, and now's the time to make his videos for colleges. He's been counting on getting accepted to a division-one school." A tear made a path down her cheek. "He's so depressed. I don't know what to do for him."

Henry looked at a loss on how to respond, and Megan felt the need to jump into the awkward silence.

"Will he be able to play eventually?"

Carolyn pursed her lips. "Yes, but who knows how this will affect his performance? He's got pins in his wrist, and the doctors say it could be six months before he's fully healed. We can't be sure about anything. His pitching days could be over."

"I'm so sorry, Carolyn." Megan touched a hand to the woman's arm.

"Thank you." The words came out in a whisper. "Henry, it's a lot to ask, but would you be willing to come by the house and talk to Joshua? Give him a pep talk? He admires you so much."

"I could do that, but are you sure that's a good idea considering what happened with my career?"

"Yes." She swiped at another tear. "You're the perfect one to talk to him. You can be the example of how to move on if things don't go as he's always planned."

He didn't look convinced that he'd be able to help. But Megan knew Carolyn was right.

"Sometimes plans change," Megan offered. "And it's not easy having a change of dreams."

Carolyn met her gaze and held it. A wry half smile curved up one side of her mouth. "You get it, Megan. Of course, you get it."

"I'd be glad to talk to your boy," Henry said.

"I can't tell you how much this means to me. Thank you," Carolyn said and then turned to Megan. "Thank you, too."

Coach Lou came into the lounge and immediately joined them. "Carolyn," he said, his tone round with concern. "How's Josh?"

"Oh, Coach, I was just telling them how he's

depressed. Fritz and I are both down about it, too, and are trying our best not to show that to our son. Josh is just so mad at himself for getting on that skateboard."

"These things happen, I'm afraid. Just glad he's okay. After he heals, he'll get some good PT, and that should help. Try not to worry."

Carolyn shook her head. "We're trying."

She said goodbye and left the lounge. After a bit of small talk with Coach Lou and Henry, Megan took the opportunity to excuse herself and go to the restroom.

Carolyn stood in front of a mirror, dabbing a tissue at the corner of her eye. Megan suddenly felt awkward alone in the space with this woman who she had previously worked hard to ignore. She thought of the moment they had just shared. The bright lights of the ladies' room gave her no place to hide.

"I thought I'd do a little repair work before I head home." Carolyn caught Megan's gaze in the mirror. "I don't want Joshua to see that I've been crying. As it is, I know he's upset about how Fritz and I reacted when it first happened. We were so disappointed in how this could affect Josh's college plans. I wish I could take back the way I behaved."

Megan said the first thing that came to her mind. "You're a good mom." She pulled her lip gloss from her purse and applied a slick to her lips, hoping the action would keep her from saying anything else. How surreal to console Carolyn Montgomery.

"You're kind, Megan." Carolyn tossed the tissue into the trash and turned to face Megan. "I'm sorry I didn't reach out to you more after William's passing. I haven't been a very good friend."

Friend? Megan wouldn't have considered them

friends. They'd been country club acquaintances and wives of men who worked in the same business office, but friends?

She didn't know how to respond to Carolyn's comment. She hadn't wanted Carolyn or any of the others from those days to reach out to her and had been relieved that they had left her alone after William died. But now she wondered if part of that adamancy had been her own sense of unbelonging. Maybe feeling as though she was on the outside of things had been because that was just where she put herself. Outside.

"The speeches should be starting any minute," Carolyn said. She uttered a soft laugh. "I worked so long and hard on this event, and handing the reins over to someone else doesn't even faze me right now." She shook her head. "I just want to go home and make sure my kid knows we've got his back no matter what. It's where I belong."

After Carolyn was gone, Megan stood alone in front of the mirror above the sink and stared at her own image. She'd wanted to feel like a genuine part of this little town, had vowed to immerse herself into the fray. And tonight at this fancy event, she knew she'd done it. She smiled at herself, met her gaze. *Don't look now, crazy. You might even like Carolyn Montgomery.*

****

Henry and Coach sat at the bar in the lounge, nursing their drinks. They'd each ordered a scotch on the rocks.

Coach circled his wrist, making the liquid in his glass spin. "I think it's good you're going to talk to the Montgomery kid. He idolizes you."

Henry snickered. "I guess he doesn't read the

tabloids."

Coach lifted his gaze from his spinning drink and focused on Henry. "Nobody around here gives one royal shit about those tabloids. Haven't you figured that out by now?"

He smiled at the older man. He'd forgotten how passionate Lou Brennen could be, how his investment in his team was contagious. And how once in a while, he swore like a sailor.

"I can't imagine you not being the high school's coach."

"It's time."

Henry nodded. "But then what?"

Coach turned to face him. His eyes were bright, his face lit up. "I've got a plan."

"Well, let's hear it."

Coach's whole body moved as he talked about the baseball camp he had always wanted to manage. He'd even investigated sites where he could house his camp. A large warehouse on the edge of town seemed like an ideal place.

"Could be a lot of work, Coach. I thought you were retiring because you wanted to slow down."

"Who said that? Can you actually see me doing jigsaw puzzles?" He snickered as he lifted his drink to his lips and took a pull. "Come on, Hank. You know me better than that."

"It's going to take some serious dough, too, isn't it?"

"I need backers." He wiggled his eyebrows.

Henry couldn't help but laugh. "Is this why you urged me to have another scotch?"

"Abso-fucking-lutely."

****

Someone on a mic announced that the speeches were about to begin. Megan made her way into the dining room and took her seat beside Lucy.

"Carolyn's not here," Lucy whispered. "Isn't this dinner her baby? Shouldn't she be the one at the microphone?"

"Carolyn had a family issue."

An older woman with gray hair up in a twist and wearing a long, straight black dress adjusted the microphone and tapped it. She thanked everyone for coming, singled out whom she referred to as "local celebrities," a group consisting of Henry Denhawk, who looked appealingly sheepish as he stood and gave the room a wave of his hand; a woman who had done a series of coffee commercials and even had a billboard with her face on it up on Route 10; and a guy who had been a regular on a soap opera until his character had been killed off.

The woman spoke about Sycamore River and how the dastardly gentrification did not mean the charm of their town would fade away. "Quite the contrary," she puffed, and a tittering sounded throughout the room.

She said roots were strong and deep in this town. The locals lived and breathed Sycamore River, and nothing would change that. Their little hamlet was an all-for-one, one-for-all kind of place, and Megan was reminded of how she'd almost not accepted the invitation to this event and how she was glad to be here.

The woman introduced the shopkeepers in town who each stood for a round of polite applause when their name was called. When it was Megan's turn, the woman explained how Megan's shop was not yet open but would be soon. As she stood, Megan couldn't help but glance toward Henry's table. His eyes were on her.

There was something about tonight. She and Henry had turned a corner as well, and she couldn't explain how or why. All she knew was that the moment he'd walked into the lounge, she wanted to be near him.

The speech concluded, and the band began to play. An old ballad wafted through the room, and couples slowly migrated to the dance floor. Megan's heart fluttered. Henry would come to ask her to dance. She knew it and didn't bother acting coy. Their dance was inevitable. She sought his gaze across the room, and he was already up from his chair and moving toward her.

She let him take her hand and guide her to the dance floor. His arm slipped around her waist and guided her closer. They danced together smoothly, the music bathing them with its sweet melody. She momentarily closed her eyes and just let herself be carried away on Henry's lead.

"That was great what you said to Carolyn before."

She opened her eyes. Henry stared at her, his head angled down, his mouth very close.

Still wrapped in the music and the feel of his body next to hers, she did not speak.

"About having a change of dreams," he reminded her.

"Oh yes. I think that's most people's experience one time or another. Having a change of dreams."

"It can be tough to do."

"It's courageous, too. Sometimes it's easier to just accept that your dream didn't come true rather than find yourself a new one."

His gaze bored into her. "What would you do if I

kissed you right now?"

She could not look away. Her mouth opened to speak, but she said nothing. The first time she had been this close to Henry, she'd been fueled by those two margaritas. Regret had flirted with her on and off ever since. But when it came down to it, she was glad. Glad to have started the chain of events that brought her to this very moment.

"I'd like to see you try." She tilted her chin up.

His mouth came down on hers gently, the kiss soft and chaste.

Until he pulled her lower lip into his mouth and sucked it.

Chapter Fifteen

"Who'd have thought that Peter Moss was such a good dancer," Lucy said as she leaned back against the driver's seat of her car. "He's got moves, I'll tell you."

Megan's mouth curved into a tired grin. "You sound smitten."

"No." Lucy tilted her head. "Just stating a fact."

"So am I."

Lucy laughed. "You should talk. Making out on the dance floor like you're at the prom."

"We weren't making out." Megan chuckled. "It was one kiss."

"One whopper of a kiss."

Megan didn't respond because to deny it would be nothing short of a lie, and to admit it would stir up too much trouble. But yes indeed. That had been one hell of a kiss, and she knew she'd relive it tonight over and over again while she tried to get to sleep.

****

The next afternoon Megan went to the coffee shop to grab a latte and a muffin before she went to the shop to get some work done.

She cleaned the dresser she'd purchased at the Laurence house sale. She removed each drawer, peeled out the contact paper, and scrubbed the wood clean with oil soap. The lemony scent was satisfying as it filled the air. She polished the brass drawer pulls and then ran a rag and furniture polish over all the wood. The piece gleamed.

The front door opened, and Henry walked in carrying a grocery bag. Interestingly, the masonry project of the back stairs had been done for days, yet Henry Denhawk continued to use her entrance to get to Sid's apartment.

"Hi," he said as he stepped inside.

"Hi." She was too glad to see him, and although she wanted to admonish herself for it, all she could do was drop her project and greet him.

"I bought some lunch. You hungry?"

"No, I had a peanut butter sandwich earlier."

"Ah, okay. I got some cheese and crackers and some grapes from the grocery. A bottle of chardonnay. Join me."

"Thanks, but you go on and enjoy. How's Sid?"

"Well, he ate some dinner—they feed supper to patients at four o'clock—and then fell asleep. A doctor came by and reported he was getting stronger, so that's good."

"Glad to hear it."

He put the bag down. "Hey, look." He reached into his shirt pocket and withdrew a small plastic bag. "The music store had phonograph needles. This one should do it."

"Wow, that was lucky." This guy had not ceased to surprise her. She thought of Lucy and her unfortunate experience with that realtor who swindled her out of a listing. Some people were good at putting on a façade. More and more she believed this Henry Denhawk to be a basically good man. The online tabloids would differ with her, she knew, but that was just gossip.

Fundamentally, he was one of the good ones. She just knew it.

"I'll take this stuff upstairs and be back down to install the needle. We can see if the thing works or not."

"Okay, that'd be great."

"Sure I can't get you a glass of wine?"

"No, thanks." Wine just turned her stomach these days. "I've got some iced tea in my thermos."

He shook his head, as if she were a lightweight. She really wasn't. Hey, she'd had two potent margaritas the night they rolled around on each other. Right now, the idea of rolling with Henry made her feel as if she'd just ridden the Tilt-A-Whirl.

While he was gone, Megan finally put away the ironing board and iron and hung all the tablecloths on a rack.

She put the tea service she purchased into a sink filled with soapy water and let it soak for a while.

Henry trotted down the back steps a little while later with an LP in his hands. It was a Sinatra album.

"I wasn't sure if you have any records, so I brought down one of Sid's. He's got a million of them."

"Yes, I know. He's pretty proud of his collection."

"Okay, let's see if we can conjure up some music."

He removed the needle from its little plastic bag and examined the phonograph's arm as though he were looking to remove a thorn from a cat's paw. Gently he inserted the needle, then plugged the machine into an outlet. He pulled the album from its jacket and placed it gingerly on the turntable.

He turned a button, and after a momentary crackling sound, Frank Sinatra crooned to them about luck being a lady tonight. Megan felt something inside her, something electric, but she wasn't sure if it was luck or pure fear. Either way, she knew she wouldn't walk away from this. Could be her feet had turned to cement.

He looked at her with a huge smile, his sky-blue eyes alight. "Success!"

She clapped, giddy with the electricity in her veins.

He extended her a hand. "Dance with me."

She eyed his outreached hand that felt somehow like a dare. If she had fallen off the side of a boat and such a hand had been offered her, the gesture would have been not just welcome but lifesaving. *Grab it.*

But what was this? She had not fallen overboard. She stood in her store, facing the handsome Henry Denhawk, and his hand, his open palm, beckoned her. She remembered their dance at the country club and the way he'd kissed her. She thumped inside, knowing another dance would produce the same result.

Maybe his gesture would not save her life, but possibly her clasping his hand would be life changing.

She watched her hand float to his, as though she were above the scene looking on and not participating in the action. His hand was large and firm, commanding yet comforting. She curled her fingers around the hand and stepped into his awaiting arms.

They moved in unison, no measured steps, and swayed to Ol' Blue Eyes' crooning about how someday he would remember how some woman looked tonight. She could identify with Frankie. Someday, she didn't know when, she would think of this night, this dance, this man, and she would be glad she took his hand when he extended it. She would not look back with an iota of regret.

"When we met," he said in a low voice.

She kept her eyes on him.

"Why did that happen?"

How many times had she tried to figure out the answer to that question? "I'm not really sure. I guess I dared myself."

"And you didn't know it was the Hawk you were flirting with in the first place?"

"No. I'd never heard of you." She smiled. "Sorry."

He smiled back. "That actually makes me glad, to tell you the truth. I like that there was just something about me that drew you toward me. I'm so sick of people putting me in a category of their own making because of who I am, or rather, who I've been. That make sense?"

"It does."

"Are you going to sell the record player or keep it?"

"I'm starting to think I'm like those women who breed dogs but then can't bear to give them away, so they keep all the puppies for themselves."

He laughed. "So you're keeping it."

"No." She shook her head. "I'm just going to make sure it goes to the right home."

"You're something." His eyes softened, filled with questions, and her heart did a little dance of its own in her chest.

He lowered his head, she lifted hers, knowing a kiss was coming, and she welcomed it, wanted it, anticipated it. His lips were soft and tender as they moved their mouths from side to side, the kiss a dance of its own. His arm circled her waist and pulled her nearer, and a soft moan sounded at the back of her throat. This was a different kiss from the night in the New York club. This was not a kiss from a daring stranger. This was a kiss from the familiar, a kiss that would not just come to mind at night when she could not sleep. This kiss would stay in her heart.

"Little did we know more than two months ago that the night in New York would lead us here."

More than two months. Had it been that long? She'd been so busy getting the Hope Chest ready that time seemed to meld into one big glob with no definition.

His kiss moved to her cheek, his soft lips brushing down the side of her face to her neck, where he lingered. Inside she was electrified. The current traveled through her system and landed somewhere low. Her heart thumped.

"Make love with me, Megan." His voice was a whisper.

Heart pounding, she was at a crossroads. She wanted to say yes, the word ready to escape her lips. But she worried, too.

The record skipped, and an unpleasant sound of the needle scraping across the vinyl disc stopped them cold. Sinatra's magic had been yanked away. Part of her charged with regret. Another part of her flooded with relief.

She bid Henry good night and went home. Residuals of their dance, the sensual, languid kiss, stayed with her, and blood rushed through her at the memory.

In her pajamas, tucked in her bed, she thought about time. In a way tonight had awakened her, made her suddenly open her eyes to place and time. She hadn't even realized she'd been in denial, that something real and scary, a truth, had settled inside her and would no longer stay quiet. Tonight, things had become clear, crystal clear.

When Lucy had taken one look at her when she'd come home, she'd asked if she was feeling all right, and Megan assured her that she was just tired. But she was more than tired. She was scared.

She knew what she had to do in the morning. It was time to make a purchase at the pharmacy.

She had to pee on a stick.

Chapter Sixteen

The next morning Lucy ran to the drugstore for her. Megan paced until her friend returned with the test. When Lucy walked in with the bag, neither woman said anything. Megan just grabbed the bag and padded into the bathroom, shutting the door.

A few minutes later Megan stared at the two pink lines in the display of the test. Her hand shook, and her insides wrenched with reality. Deep down she knew it, but seeing the confirmation in those two pink lines just rocked her. She was pregnant.

She and Henry Denhawk had made a baby on their one fateful night together. What the hell was she going to do now?

She emerged from the bathroom and went into the kitchen, where her best friend stood waiting, braced against the counter, arms folded. She unfurled her fingers to reveal the wand in her hand.

"Oh, sweetie," Lucy said. "I had no idea."

"How could you? I didn't mention a thing to you, but I've suspected for a little while. I was kind of in denial, too. Lucy, what am I going to do? As much as I've wanted to have a child, I'm freaking out. How can I raise a baby?" She laughed an incredulous sound. "All those years when William and I tried to conceive and nothing. We kept our hopes up for so long, but eventually we just figured it was not our lot in life. Now look at me. Dear God." She put her face in her hands. "Now I'm alone."

"First off, you are not alone. That little darling you're carrying is my niece or nephew, and I plan on being a big part of that kid's life. I mean, was I born to be somebody's cool aunt or what?"

She smiled at her friend. Thank God for Lucy. "I don't think I should tell Henry."

"You have to."

"Why?"

"Because he's going to be a father. That's why."

"But he can't wait to get back to his own life. He's got this job he's been dying to snag, and it looks like it might happen for him, and then I'm going to swoop in and say 'well, wait just a minute, buster'?"

"No. Of course not. But he still needs to know."

She closed her eyes again. She hoped that the right thing to do would come to her.

"I've got this young couple I'm showing a house to. Newlyweds looking to buy their first house. They're so stinking cute. But I can cancel if you need me to."

"No, Lucy. You go on and meet your clients. There's nothing we can do now."

She thought of her adventure with Henry at the Laurence house sale, their walk along River Road, and their looking in the windows of the cottage for sale. Their lighthearted enthusiasm for that house's potential had been fun. Henry's ideas for remodeling gave his eyes an appealing sparkle. How was she going to look into those blue eyes of his and tell him he was going to be a father? Surprise!

Lucy put on a woolen blazer and grabbed her messenger bag. "What are you planning to do while I'm gone?"

Megan shrugged. "Pace."

She squeezed Megan's hand. "We've got this."

If she remained alone in the house, her mind would shift into overdrive. Every scenario she conjured up ended with her being hurt and scared. She grabbed her jacket and fished her key fob from her purse. She had to get out of here.

She drove to the Hope Chest, needing to be there in that space. She looked around her store. Her work had really paid off. She could open the store today if she had to. She still had a couple of boxes of things to unpack and clean up, but for the most part she had enough merchandise to entice customers. Her heart did a dance. All this anticipation and she was almost ready to open her doors.

She gingerly ran a hand over her still-flat abdomen. There was a baby in there. A miracle. William would have been so pleased. Guilt settled in her chest and squeezed her heart. She sure had a knack for doing things the hard way.

She made an appointment with her doctor, then did her best to immerse herself into work, being mindful not to lift anything too heavy. At her age a pregnancy was high risk, and she was amazed at how, now that she knew for sure about the baby, she had become a tiger mom to this minuscule being growing inside her.

She unpacked a box of board games she'd purchased at a rummage sale, and she sat on an area rug and checked each one to see if all the pieces were inside each box. The only memories she had of playing board games as a kid were of her watching families on TV and wishing she were a part of them. She'd watched

The Brady Bunch over and over, wondering what it could possibly be like to have a group of people around that belonged to her, warts and all. Not that the Bradys had many warts. Their fights involved one kid teasing another kid, and their mom or housekeeper intervened by telling them things like "No pudding for you tonight." Her time living with Aunt Gemma did not include board games, and for damn sure she hadn't had pudding for dessert.

She figured most people nowadays played games on their phones, but she guessed that sometimes it would be fun to play Monopoly.

The day unfolded. She walked to the diner and had a bowl of oatmeal for lunch, then she went over to Elaine and Joe's Candy and Confections to buy some candy for customers on Halloween. The milk chocolate ghosts were really cute, and she planned on stapling one of her business cards to the cellophane wrappers. She'd give these to adults. For kids she purchased a large bag of mini chocolate bars and would put them in the pumpkin-designed bowl she had for just that purpose.

After dropping off her purchases, she went to the flower shop and bought one red rose. She had let two Fridays go by without visiting William. She needed to go there today.

The walk to the cemetery was brisk but refreshing. She meandered along the aisle to William's grave and placed the long-stemmed rose onto the flat top of the granite.

She stared at his name and sighed.

"I'm going to have a baby, William. I know it's crazy, right? I mean who starts having a family when they're almost forty?" She tried to laugh, but tears came to her eyes instead. "I know how much you wanted children. I gave up that dream a long time ago.

"I won't give you all the details of how this happened, but please know that I have recently discovered that I care very much for this baby's father. When I first found out I was pregnant, I debated on even telling him, but standing here right now talking to you, I've decided I have to. Henry—that's his name—should know.

"I don't believe Henry and I will be parents together like you and I would have been. I see no marriage for him and me. But I do know enough about him that he will do right by this child. My child will know his father. That much I know. The rest of it?" She shrugged. "Not a clue."

She kissed her hand and touched her fingertips to the cold granite where William's name was etched, and she left. Silently she thanked William for giving her the direction she needed.

At the store Megan settled herself in her back room and put her feet up for a little while. Lucy called to check on her, and she assured her that she was still keeping herself busy and would be home for dinner. She just felt like being alone right now. Not that she was sorting out her thoughts in any way. Right now too many things to think about sat like a ball of tangled yarn in her head. No beginning, no end, just crisscrossing strands going everywhere and making no sense.

As dusk settled in, she realized she hadn't heard from nor seen Henry all day. Not that she expected to, but she'd gotten used to seeing him. She remembered that he was in the city today at that meeting he'd told her about. He really wanted that contract as a baseball commentator. How would her news affect him if he got the job? She couldn't think that far.

After last night's restlessness, she finally put her head back on the small sofa and closed her eyes. Sleep claimed her immediately.

"Hello."

She woke with a start. It was dark outside. What time was it? She bolted up at the sound of Henry's voice.

"Back here," she responded. She stood up from the sofa and ran a hand over her hair.

A moment later he entered her room, standing there in a sports jacket and dress pants, a button-down shirt and blue paisley tie. He looked as if he belonged on the cover of a magazine. Her heart rose, then fell. He was so appealing, more attractive than the guy she'd first seen at the club in New York. That had been a stranger. She knew this guy, and this guy made her knees weak.

She smoothed her hands over her clothes, wondering if she looked as disheveled as she felt.

"I must have dozed off for a minute. What time is it?"

He smiled at her, a dazzlingly bright smile so genuine her heart started to crack. "After five."

"Wow. How did your meeting go?"

"I got the job, Megan."

"What?"

"The Mets want me. I'm in."

"Oh my God," she said and instinctively threw her arms around him.

He squeezed her close, lifting her off the floor. He swung her around. "Can you believe it?"

"I'm so happy for you, Henry." The words caught in her throat, although she genuinely was glad for him, knowing how much this chance meant to him.

She had developed feelings for this man who weeks ago had been nothing but a handsome stranger. Now she was moved beyond words at his good news. Her news, however, would have to wait, although her trip to the cemetery today had convinced her that she had to tell Henry the truth. Now was not the time.

"My head's spinning." He put her down and released his hold on her. "I've got so many things buzzing around in my head. I mean, I explained the whole thing about Sid to the board, and they were very understanding. They know I can't just go to New York right now and turn my back on the situation. So my start date is up in the air at the moment, and my lawyer's got to go over the details of the contract, but verbally we have a deal."

"Wow." This was his dream. His dreams did not include her or her secret, and that realization gave her a pang. But there would be time to talk that through.

His cell phone rang, and he started to laugh. "My agent's blowing up my phone. If it's possible, he's more excited than I am." Without looking at the screen, he swiped to connect the call.

"Hi," he said and winked at her.

His face blanched. A twinge of concern trickled into her veins. She put her hand on her belly, surprising herself at the instinctive move. She studied his face and waited.

"Okay, yes, of course. Yes."

He ended the call and stared at her. On instinct, her breath locked in her throat.

"Megan, I've got to go. That was the hospital. It's Sid."

Chapter Seventeen

The elevator cab was full, and Henry had to wait for the next one. He pushed the button a dozen times even though the light was on, indicating that another elevator was on its way. Taking its sweet time.

Finally, the bell dinged, and the doors opened. He hopped in and pushed the button for Sid's floor. It was almost seven o'clock, well after regular hours. Something was definitely wrong. They wouldn't tell him over the phone, only that they "suggested" he get here as soon as possible. His insides hurt from the way he was clenching. He was cold. Did they keep this place like a refrigerator for a reason? His lightweight jacket did him no good.

The doors opened, and he made his way to the desk. A nurse he did not recognize, an older woman with her hair in a fat gray braid, looked up when he approached.

"Hi, I'm Henry Denhawk. I'm here to see my stepfather, Sid Goldman."

A flash of something he didn't understand flickered across her eyes, and she asked him to wait a moment while she made a call. Who was she calling? What was going on?

A moment later Sid's neurologist, Winifred Harold, padded down the hallway. "Hello, Henry." Her voice was warm, sympathetic. "Come with me, would you?"

He followed her to a room off the main corridor. It appeared to be a small waiting room where a TV was affixed high on the wall and was tuned to the weather channel. They were talking rain sometime in the beginning of the week. Magazines arranged like a fan crowded the surface of a small laminate table. Empty chairs stood in a perfect row.

"Henry, Sid's had another stroke."

"Oh." His stomach folded over itself, and he felt as if he was going to throw up. "How bad is it?"

"We're still testing, but it appears as though this was a bigger one than last time."

"Is he...?"

"He's not conscious, but his heart rate is steady, and although it's slow, it's not a danger. His blood pressure is coming down with medication. We're monitoring him, and as I said, we're doing some tests to see what we're dealing with. For now, though, we're letting him rest so he can gain some more strength."

Henry ran a hand through his hair. He hadn't expected this. Sid was supposed to go to a rehab where he could happily boss people around.

"Would you like to see him?"

"See him? Can I?"

"Sure. But he's unconscious, and it's best if you don't try to wake him this time. His body and his brain need the rest."

"I understand."

"Thank you for coming. Keep the faith, Henry. Sid's a tough old bird. There's every chance he'll rebound from this like he did last time."

He nodded, thanked her, and went down the

hallway to Sid's room.

Sid lay with an oxygen mask over his mouth and nose. A constant hissing sound came from a new machine. He was hooked up to more monitors than he had been before. Everything was lit up with digits that meant God knew what.

Henry watched Sid's chest slowly rise and fall with each breath. He soundlessly approached the bed. Sid was pale, almost gray, his cheeks sunken in. *Holy shit*. He swallowed what felt like a handful of nails.

Dr. Harold had asked him to be quiet, not to wake Sid from this needed sleep. He found himself thinking of what he'd say to Sid if he were awake. Maybe he'd tell him the news of his job offer. He'd definitely let him know that his cat, Mookie, was thriving and taking his nightly medicine like a champ. Out of nowhere his mind spoke to Sid.

Be a champ, Sid. He didn't know where the thought came from, nor did he understand the ache behind his nose or the blurriness of his vision. An image of happier times came to his head. His mother was alive then, and Sid was glad to hear Henry's news that he'd been drafted to the Mets as a member of their bullpen. Andrew was still alive, too, but weak and lying on the sofa, an avocado-green, crocheted afghan draped over his long, skinny body.

That day Sid gave him some advice. "Always remember to be a champion," he said and went on to say that champions were the best they could be in whatever their circumstances.

Maybe Henry wouldn't begin his tenure as a starting pitcher, and maybe he'd wind up being a closer or a relief guy, but wherever he was needed, Sid told him to be a champion at it. Then he turned to the figure reclined on the sofa, and he winked at his son, which made Andrew grin. They all knew that Andrew's predicament sucked, but he was still positive from day to day, still cheerful even when he had to go to the hospital for tests or an injection. He'd been a true champion.

He studied the old man's face now in the dimly lit hospital room and looked for any sign of awareness that Henry was there at his bedside. None came.

A while later he left Sid's room and approached the desk again. The same braided-haired nurse was there, her face kind.

"Someone will contact me if there's any change?" he asked.

"Of course."

"Thanks."

He turned to walk away, and the nurse with the braid wished him a good night.

As he was about to push the button for the elevator, a nurse or a doctor—he didn't know which—called out to him.

"Mr. Denhawk," the young man said. "Can you wait a moment?"

Behind the young man Henry spied Winifred Harold scurrying down the hallway in the direction of Sid's room with other personnel in lab coats. Something inside him crashed in on itself as if he'd been a victim of a hit-and-run.

An intern escorted him to that small waiting room where the weather channel droned on about the impending rain on the horizon.

"What's happening?"

"I'm not sure, but Dr. Harold asked me to have you wait."

"Okay."

Henry sat in one of the hard-plastic chairs. He stared at the weather channel screen, the woman in a blue dress yammering about warming trends and upcoming winter projections. It all ran together, and he was getting a headache. All he could do was wait.

****

Sid Goldman died. Henry let the news settle in his brain and tried to muster a sense of belief. It did not feel real. Another stroke had come swiftly upon Sid from left field and done him in. Winifred Harold could not have been nicer or more gracious when she came into the waiting room, sat beside Henry in one of the uncomfortable chairs, and told him the news.

He didn't know what to say. All he could do was thank her for all she'd done. What else was there?

Arrangements were being made by the hospital, and they asked him for a name of a funeral home. All he knew was the one where they had gone for his mother, McCallister Funeral Home, in Sycamore River. He told her as much and watched as she jotted the name onto a page on a small pad.

The parking garage was almost empty when he went to his truck, the only vehicle in a long row of unused parking places, and the lot's near-vacant state gave the low-ceilinged, cavernous space an eerie, lonely feel. He closed his eyes. Everything was eerie right now.

He drove back to Sid's apartment and didn't know if he was glad or disappointed that Megan had left for the night. She'd stuck a sticky note on Sid's door.

"Hope all is well," her note said. "Call me if you need anything."

Did he need anything? Yes. He needed to hear Megan's voice.

Chapter Eighteen

Megan fell asleep with her cell phone in her hand, and when it buzzed in her palm, she started.

She immediately connected the call. "Hello?"

"Megan." Henry's voice stalled.

She switched the phone to her other ear as she sat up straighter and waited for him to continue.

Finally, his words met her ears. "Sid died tonight."

"Oh God."

"Another stroke."

Her stomach roiled. "I'm so sorry." Tears came to her eyes. She'd been prone to them lately. "How are you?"

"Numb, I think."

His voice was low, almost a whisper, and she couldn't tell if it was the pain of loss that gave his tone its register or if he was fatigued.

"Was he gone when you got to the hospital?"

"No. He was in a coma when I got there. He passed a little while later. As I was leaving, actually."

So he hadn't had a chance to say goodbye, if he'd been so inclined. She knew that Henry and Sid's relationship was not good, yet something connected the two men, even if it was just their love for Henry's mother.

"Is there anything I can do, Henry?"

"No. But thanks. It was just good to hear your

voice."

They ended the call, and she stared at the ceiling. What must be going on in his mind right now? How would he process this?

Her bedside clock said it was just after one o'clock. She threw off her covers and scrambled for a pair of socks and her sneakers. Her nightclothes—plaid flannel pajama pants and a long-sleeved T-shirt with the picture of a triple-decker ice cream cone emblazoned on the front—would have to do.

She pulled on a jacket, jotted a quick note to Lucy, and went downstairs to grab her purse and car key. She wouldn't let herself think about what she was doing and where she was going. She just went.

She parked in front of her store and went in, disabled the alarm. Padding across the old wooden floor, she made her way to the back and climbed the stairs. She rapped her knuckles lightly on the apartment door. From the road she'd seen a light on in the back of the apartment, which must have been Henry's bedroom.

Her heart beat rapidly, and her mind refused to think through whether showing up in her pajamas was a good or bad idea. She was here, and that was that.

When he didn't respond, she turned the knob, and the door opened. Mookie came running to greet her and gave a soft mew. She ran her hand over the cat and looked around. She'd been right. The light she'd seen from the window was down the hallway in one of the bedrooms. She softly made her way to him.

Henry sat on the end of a bed of honeyed vintage maple. He was in boxers and a white T-shirt. His blond head was bent down as if he were in prayer. A lump grew in her throat.

He slowly lifted his head, and his eyes brightened. "You came." He pushed up from the bed and moved toward her.

"I, uh, had to give you something."

His one word was a whisper. "What?"

She pressed close to him and wrapped her arms around his neck. She pulled him into a tight embrace. They stayed like that for a long moment, wrapped in the protection of their closeness.

When they broke apart, he gave her a half smile. "Thank you."

"Think you'll get some sleep?"

He shrugged. "That's the plan, I guess. If I can shut my mind off, that is."

"How about I stay for a while?"

He cast his gaze over her, and his mouth curved into a rueful smile. "You are dressed for the occasion."

"Come on. Get in under the covers. I'll hang around until you fall asleep."

He did as he was told and slipped into bed. She went around to the other side of the bed and climbed in under the sheet and comforter. She scrunched closer to him.

He reached down and grabbed hold of her hand. "Thank you for this."

She squeezed his hand and listened to him settle deeper against his pillow. His rhythmic breathing was like a metronome that normally would have lulled her to sleep. But this big man next to her was suffering in a way she could not define, and all she could do was stare into the darkness and think about what lay ahead for him in the next few days.

Finally, though, she did sleep and then woke with a

start, momentarily disoriented. She focused her gaze on the man next to her. He was awake and staring at her. During their sleep they had gravitated closer to each other, each on their side facing the other.

"Did you sleep?" she whispered.

"A little."

"Better than nothing."

He tucked a strand of her hair behind her ear. She reached for his wrist and held his hand in place, his fingers still on her hair.

He scooted closer and pulled her to him. "I can't tell you what it meant to me that you came here tonight."

She nuzzled him and drew in his familiar scent. He stroked her hair, his hand running down her back. He tucked her closer still.

She lifted her face toward his, their lips a breath apart. Their gazes locked, and he bent down and softly kissed her mouth. She returned the kiss, slid her arms up and around his shoulders. She pushed away all thoughts of the news she had to deliver to him eventually. This was not the time for that, nor was it time to discuss funeral arrangements and what would come with all that.

In the darkness Henry appeared young and vulnerable, and Megan's heart lurched with affection. Staring deeply at him, she slowly pulled her T-shirt up and off. She tossed the garment to the floor. She did the same with her flannel pajama pants. Henry's eyes shone with questions; his lips parted.

She gently took his hand and brought it to her breast, cupping his fingers around the mound. When she released his hand, he let it delicately trail down her skin, grazing along her form and forcing alive every cell of her being.

After tugging off his own nightwear, he pulled her into his embrace, pressed against her skin on skin, and kissed her neck.

"You're so beautiful," he whispered.

They kissed again. He touched her with exploring hands, caring hands, needy hands. Her heart hammered in her chest as she let her fingers run along the length of his arm. He was such a strong man, taut and muscular. But what compelled her now to reach for him was the vulnerability she'd come to recognize like an old friend. It called to her like a siren.

Slowly Henry shifted, rolling gently on top of her. He uttered a soft groan as he entered her. She gasped, welcoming him. They moved together, a dance of love and comfort and abandon, and with arms wrapped tightly, she held on to him. She closed her eyes, and a single tear slipped from under a lid. Somewhere in the night she had fallen in utter, irrevocable love with Henry Denhawk.

Later they snuggled close. Periodically he kissed her temple, and each time her heart called to him. She'd tried to stay away from this man, tried to tell herself that her pregnancy was something she would deal with on her own, without him. But a shift had taken place. A seismic shift.

They slept, and as light began its ascent on the horizon, they awoke in each other's arms.

She dreaded the moment either one of them would break the magic spell of the bed's cocoon. But it was a new day, and Megan had no idea what was in store.

Chapter Nineteen

Henry hated to leave Megan, but he had a meeting at the funeral home at nine o'clock. When he came out of the shower, she had made the bed and put on her pajamas from last night. He still couldn't believe this beautiful, genuine woman had shared his bed and shared his conflicted grief. He didn't know how to process this or anything that happened in the past twenty-four hours. He embraced her—there were no words from him or her. To him, anything he said would pale compared to what was going on inside him. He kissed her hand and left to meet the funeral director.

He went through the motions with the director of McCallister Funeral Home, making selections that were just blind guesses. What did he know about what Sid would have wanted? He did his best, and that would have to be good enough.

The director took much of the burden off Henry's shoulders by contacting the newspapers, reaching out to the cemetery where Sid would join his son, Andrew, in their double grave positioned beside Henry's mother's plot.

He made arrangements for a repast at the Admiral Hotel, but when the person in charge there asked him about how many guests he'd be expecting, he was clueless. Did Sid have friends? He didn't know. Certainly, people hadn't come on Henry's behalf. Even people who knew he had come back to town wouldn't be considered friends. For all he knew, he'd be alone beside that old man's casket.

****

Megan could not believe the end of the month was here already. Halloween was in five days. Five! Was she really ready to open her doors? She surprised herself by touching her belly when she felt a twinge of worry or anticipation. It was as though her baby were giving her support. She didn't know this person growing inside her, but she loved him or her already. And she loved her baby's father.

While she finished up some things at the store, her mind was on Henry and the tasks he had to tackle today. Her heart was with him. She thought about last night, the love they'd made, the closeness they'd shared. She closed her eyes and relived the moments, one by one.

Last night was not the first time she'd lain with Henry Denhawk. She and the man had had sex two months ago, fast, hot, unabashed sex. Last night was nothing like that. Last night had been rapture. Need met want, comfort met pleasure, desire met love.

She had to stop this. She didn't even know what Henry was thinking. For all she knew, he could have viewed their lovemaking as a repeat performance from that random night in the city. She swallowed hard. *Oh, please don't let him think about it that way.*

Megan washed and dried a box of stoneware dishes she had bought a while ago. She stacked the set on top of a display table and labeled the set for sale. She felt a twinge in her insides and a momentary stab of pain in her groin, and her hand went right to her belly. Maybe she was doing too much. She had to remember she wasn't alone in this anymore.

She locked up the store early and went home and hoped she'd hear from Henry. Later that night she received a text from him, telling her everything was settled with the funeral.

She wished she'd heard his voice. Maybe the sound would have erased the doubt that crept into her bones the way winter slowly took over the atmosphere. And like winter, doubt couldn't be stopped once it began.

Chapter Twenty

McCallister Funeral Home was on the town square, and parking was a bitch. Megan parked her vehicle in a pharmacy lot across the street and walked to the building.

A man in a suit greeted her as she came in through the doorway. A wooden stand inside the viewing room was set up with an open book and a pen for guests to sign in. She picked up the pen and wrote her name on the next available line on the page.

She was surprised to see that the room was filled with mourners. She recognized some people, others no. Henry, in a suit and tie, stood up at the front by the open casket. Her insides did a flip at the sight of Sid.

She and Henry locked eyes. In a moment, though, someone came up to him and grabbed his attention.

Lucy walked in and slipped her arm through Megan's.

"Hi, you."

"Hi, you."

"Have you gone up there yet?"

"No, I just got here."

"I'm waiting for Peter."

Megan's mouth curved into a smile. "You two are adorable."

"Stop it." But Lucy leaned in close to Megan and whispered in her ear. "Who knew I'd be such a nerd fan?"

They shared a quick hug, then Megan walked up to the front of the room.

****

Henry was blown away by the people that came. The room was filled with members of the community, and what stunned him was Coach Lou. He came in with many of Sycamore River High School's varsity baseball team. These boys had met Henry when he stopped by the batting cages and gave them some advice on their technique. Now here they were, teenage boys with lots of better things to do, he was sure, paying their respects to an old man they most likely did not know.

"Coach." Henry shook the man's hand. "I can't believe you're here with the team."

"They wanted to come," Lou said. "I asked, and they said yes. No hesitation."

He cast his gaze to the boys, all with expectation on their young faces. "Thank you, guys, for coming. This is really nice of all of you."

Some nodded, some fist bumped him, and some mouthed "you're welcome." They were a scrappy bunch, the same as he and his team had been back in the day. He didn't know these boys from Adam, but he had the distinct impression that they were good kids. Even the ones that sometimes gave their coach a run for his money.

His gaze riveted to Megan as she slowly made her way through the clusters of people. As she got closer, his pulse quickened. Her eyes were so filled with affection he had to catch himself before he pulled her into his arms. What was it with this woman? All he wanted was to be in her orbit, to be where she was, to feel her warmth and honesty.

Megan discreetly gave him a quick kiss on the cheek and squeezed his hand.

"How are you holding up?" she whispered.

He recognized the floral scent of her perfume and breathed her in. "I'm overwhelmed with how many people are here. I mean, is it possible Sid knew all these folks?"

"Maybe." She scanned the crowd, then met his gaze again. "I think some of these folks remember who you are and want to support you."

He opened his mouth to speak and closed it again for fear of what he'd say. He had an odd sensation in his throat.

One by one, people came up to him to offer their condolences. Carolyn Montgomery and her husband came to pay their respects, and she was quick to thank him for giving their son, Joshua, a call.

"With all you've got going on, it was so nice of you to reach out to our son," she said.

"My pleasure." The kid might have pins in his wrist, but he had a better attitude than Henry'd had when he busted himself up skiing. Their sixteen-year-old seemed wiser than he'd ever been. "I told him I'd touch base with him again."

Some attendees had to introduce themselves because many of them he'd never seen. They told Henry how they had known Sid, and others, as Megan had said, told him how they were there for Henry and how they remembered him. One woman had been in his high school graduating class and reminded him that he'd fixed her up with a classmate who was now her husband. She said he was out of town and couldn't be here now, but he sent his condolences.

An older couple reminded him that he used to mow their lawn when he was a teenager. They shared a couple of anecdotes and seemed genuinely fond of the time he'd been in their company.

Men from the town's senior group surrounded him. These were Sid's cronies.

"So at last we meet the Hawk," one of the old guys said. He clapped Henry on the shoulder. "Sid liked to complain about you, but he sure knew all your stats and could rattle them off at will."

"Could he?"

"Sure."

A local minister said a few words. Apparently, Sid had been involved in their soup kitchen. He'd volunteered on Wednesday afternoons, and he was faithful to that schedule. It was as if they were talking about a person he'd never met, and in some way that made him sad.

The interment at the cemetery was quick, and the funeral director said a few nice and moving words. At the end of the service, the funeral director invited those in attendance to join in a repast at the Admiral Hotel.

****

Several local store owners came to the repast, and Megan had the chance to speak with them about the open-house event the stores would be participating in by giving out candy, caramel apples, hot cocoa, and other goodies. She felt welcome among them, as if she were a new member of some club. They offered support as she faced the opening of the Hope Chest.

"Call me anytime," one woman said.

"I'll stop in and see how you're doing," said another.

The Hope Chest was already working its magic.

Megan kept her eye on Henry during the luncheon. She watched him interact with his guests. She liked his easy smile and the way he appeared engaged in the conversations he shared. He'd make a good commentator for major league baseball. People liked him. They listened when he spoke.

A warmth surged through her as she watched Henry. He seemed glad to speak with his former high school coach and the kids on the team who had come to the luncheon as well. He engaged with the kids, who hung on every word he had to say. He was a natural, she decided, and his pursuit of the new position with the Mets organization was something he had to do. Nothing could stand in his way. Her heart did a little blip. What would he say when he learned she was having his baby? *Please don't view our baby as an obstacle.*

Her hand floated to her belly. When would she tell Henry? No time ever seemed right.

"Nice crowd," a male voice said.

She turned to see that Henry's agent had kind of sneaked up on her. "Yes. I'm pleased for Henry."

"You're the tenant, the one opening a shop downtown, right?"

"Yes. Megan Harris."

"Cliff Jordan." He turned his attention to Henry. "Your friend is all set to embark on a major career move. Has he mentioned that to you?"

"Yes." Something about this man put her on edge. She felt as if she were being interrogated, which put her on the defensive and had her responding in a minimum number of words.

"Yeah, he's one lucky guy," Cliff continued to say. "Not too many people get second chances in his kind of business."

She didn't comment on that statement, because she didn't like his implication.

He took a sip of a pilsner of beer. "Nice seeing you, Megan." He turned to walk away, then paused and smiled at her. "You're much prettier in person."

What the hell did that mean? She watched Cliff make his way across the room, his eyes seeming to study everyone and everything in his path.

Later, as the crowd thinned, Megan scanned the room. Henry was alone at the bar, nursing a short glass of some dark brown liquid. Between sips he ran a finger around the rim of the glass, his gaze riveted to the task.

She slipped onto the stool beside him. "Hey, you."

He lifted his head and offered a tepid smile. "Hey."

"Long day, huh?"

He nodded, took a sip of his drink.

"You okay, Henry?"

He let out an audible breath, looked up at the ceiling, then met her gaze. "Sid's lawyer just informed me that the estate has been left solely to me. I'm still trying to wrap my brain around the news."

She didn't know what to say. Based on things Henry had said about his relationship with Sid, she could see why he was surprised.

"I'm kind of shocked right now, you know? I mean, he and I hadn't spoken to each other in years. We parted under bad circumstances. Why on earth would that man make sure I got his estate?"

"Maybe he drew up the will long before you two had an issue?"

He shook his head. "The will was amended a year after I left town. We were still not speaking at that time. Hell, we were only in each other's company due to his health crisis."

"He must have cared after all?"

He stared at her for a moment, then shook his head. "I'm starting to think everything's screwed up." He kept his gaze focused forward, as though he were trying to choose from the lineup of libations on the shelf behind the bar. "Does it help?"

"Does what help?"

"When you talk to someone when you know they can't hear you or can't answer you like you were doing in the cemetery that day?"

"Who says I don't get an answer? I mean, no, William's voice doesn't come blasting into my ears like from some divine speaker, but on some inner-gut level, I hear him. And I believe he hears me. Is that what you mean?"

He didn't answer, kept his eyes focused on the display on the bar's shelves.

"It's a matter of faith, Henry."

He nodded. "I'm tired."

"Need me to drive you home?"

His mouth curved into a rueful smile. "I'm good."

"Okay, then. I'm going to get some rest as well. I have a big day coming. The opening of the Hope Chest is on Friday."

"You excited?"

"Scared, too, but yes. It's what I've wanted and dreamed of for so long." She paused for a moment, then added, "Like you and your offer from the Mets. Despite what's happening with other things, it's satisfying."

He met her gaze. "Thank you for being here today."

She touched a hand to his arm. *I wouldn't be anywhere else.* "Of course."

****

Later, Megan threw on a sweats outfit and relaxed. It had been a long, tiring day, and it just felt good to shed her skirt with the too-snug waist where the poor strained button had dug into her flesh.

She thought about the conversation she had with Henry. The man was doing some soul searching. His troubled look made her heart thump. What emotions was he experiencing? Would he let her in?

Lucy was out with Peter. She was alone in the house and decided to go to Lucy's room to grab a view of herself in her cheval mirror. She stood sideways and examined her silhouette. Was her midsection protruding a little? She pulled the fabric of her top taut. Yes, maybe it was. Her heart did a flip. She had to tell Henry.

She hated having to give him this news after what he'd been through in the past couple of days.

But it was time.

Her cell phone rang, and she dashed to her room to get the call. She hoped it was Henry. But the display showed an unfamiliar number. She swiped to connect the call. "Hello?"

"Hello, baby doll."

Megan's heart stopped at the gravelly smoker's voice of her aunt Gemma. It had been years since she'd talked with her despite the checks she faithfully sent each month.

"Cat got your tongue? Huh, girl?" Gemma had been drinking. She was looking for a fight.

"What is it you want, Gemma?"

"That any way to greet the person who raised you? The only person on earth who gave two shits about what happened to you? I taught you better than that."

Taught me? Megan's chest ached. Gemma hadn't been around when Megan needed help with homework or someone to cook her a hot meal or provide her with clean clothes. She had been in charge of her own existence from the time she could reach the stove.

"How about you just tell me why it is you're calling me?"

She could hear Gemma taking a long drink of something. Gemma was a beer drinker and could typically polish off a twelve-pack in no time.

"Saw that you got yourself a nice new boyfriend. He's a looker. I'll tell you that."

"What?" Megan pressed the phone to her ear. "What are you talking about?"

"It was pointed out to me that there are pictures of you and this new dreamboat on the internet. Had to see for myself." Gemma uttered a long chuckle, then broke out into a coughing fit. She was still smoking. "Then I did a little checking. You caught yourself a big fish, didn't you?"

"What pictures, Gemma?"

"Google. My friend Paulie showed me."

Megan grabbed her laptop from her nightstand and opened the lid. She fired it up and typed her name into the search field. Up popped a series of snapshots of her with Henry from the country club dance looking all cozied up next to each other like a couple. Who had taken these shots? Did Henry requisition these? Her heart sank. This must be what Henry's agent had meant when he made that comment about her looking prettier in person.

"So in light of your new situation, I'm calling to let you know that the two hundred dollars you been sending me ain't cutting it these days. Inflation, you know."

She should never have started to give her aunt money each month. The sad thing was that she had felt sorry for her in that ratty old shack on the outskirts of Chicago. The power was always being shut off, and she'd call Megan in a panic, and she'd have to wire money to pay the arrearage. Sending a monthly check had just been easier and more efficient. But that hadn't been the only reason. The honest truth cut like a knife.

"How about it, baby doll? I was thinking I could get by with you doubling the amount."

"That's not going to happen, Gemma. I've got a lot on my plate these days."

"With that thrift shop you're opening? Yeah, I know about that, too." She snickered. "You and your hoity-toity life. You can afford a lot more than I'm asking for."

"That's not true."

Gemma was silent for a long moment; Megan could hear her phlegmy breathing. Had she dozed off?

"What is true, baby girl, is that the truth about you could turn your tidy little life upside down. You think about that?"

Ire coursed through Megan's veins. She'd been extorted by this person who was her only living relative, the one the government paid money for her to raise Megan. Almost none of that money had gone to Megan's care. Megan had gotten her first job bussing tables when she was eleven.

When her parents died, her father's only sister had taken her in. And her life had been nothing short of miserable. She was sick of Gemma Lang and her demands and her threats. Sick to death of her.

"I'm hanging up now, Gemma. It's late."

"I'd think long and hard, missy."

She ended the call and threw the phone across her bed.

Chapter Twenty-One

Megan stood with her new hire, Mandy, a college student from Montclair, at the register and went over the pricing index and other functions of the machine.

"I can't believe how much you've got done since the day I came in for the interview."

Megan scanned the store with new eyes, excited that her dream of the Hope Chest was ready.

She showed Mandy the merchandise as they made their way around the space. She explained that all prices for items were negotiable and that Mandy should run any of those barters by her.

"If I'm not here with you, I'm a cell phone away. Just give me a call if you need anything."

The memory of her phone call with her aunt taunted Megan. The drunkard's attempt to milk more funds from her made her sick, and the woman's dangling the threat of exposing Megan's past was just proof that Gemma Lang had no real feelings for her whatsoever.

"Will do," Mandy said. "The place really looks great. The hope chest looks wonderful and really catches the eye when you walk by the store."

She liked that her employee seemed to have a good eye for esthetics. Megan had liked her the moment they met and was glad the girl was on board.

"You're keeping the cabinet locked, I see."

"Not by choice, I'm afraid." Megan made a face. "I locked it, then proceeded to lose the key."

"That stinks."

Megan's mouth twisted to the side. "I'm going to have to give in and call a locksmith."

Mandy nodded as if she understood that Megan had still held out a fragment of hope for the key to show up in a pocket or something.

"So we'll open at ten o'clock on Halloween, and you and I will both be here. We hand out the business cards attached to the candy ghosts to adults, and all the kiddies can pick any candy bar they'd like from the bucket at the desk. I got us each a witch's hat so we can be festive. That sound good?"

"Perfect."

"If you could take the polishing cloth and go over the items on that table there, that would be great. I'm just going into the back room for a few."

"Got it." Mandy went right to work.

Everything regarding the shop was falling into place. Megan's insides fluttered, and then a strange pulling sensation hit her in her belly. When she stepped into the back room, she sat on the sofa and breathed through her mouth. Was this just her nerves? Last night's phone call had kept her awake until late in the night. Maybe she was just tired. She felt sweaty and jittery. Had to be nerves. Anticipation was understandable.

"Hey, girls," Lucy called out from the store. "I bring coffee and sustenance from Java Joe's."

A moment later Lucy came into the back room where Megan emerged from the bathroom. Lucy took one look at Megan's face and dashed to her side.

"Sweetie, what's wrong? You look pale."

"I just checked. I'm spotting."

"Did you call your doctor?"

"Um." She fiddled with her phone. "Doing that right now."

Megan punched in her obstetrician's number. She explained the situation to the nurse, then waited while the message was relayed to the doctor. Lucy stood by, hands in fists, as though ready to jump into action.

When the call ended, Megan's eyes filled with tears. She looked at her friend. "She wants me to come in right away."

"I'll take you."

"Where are we going?"

Both women turned to the voice coming from the entrance to the room. Henry. His mouth set in a frown, eyes intent, he assessed the scene.

Lucy and Megan exchanged a look.

"Megan's not feeling well, and I'm taking her to her doctor."

Henry came closer and captured her gaze. "Megan, what's happening?"

She hadn't wanted to do it this way. She took a shaky breath. "I'm pregnant."

His eyes widened, but he said nothing.

"And, um, I have a problem."

"What kind of problem?"

"The doctor wants to examine me."

"Okay, then." He scooped her up into his arms.

"What are you doing?"

"Taking you to your doctor."

"Henry, put me down."

"No can do."

He made his way from that back room and through the store. Mandy and Lucy stood together as he carried her out the door.

"Call me," Lucy shouted after them.

He placed her in the passenger seat of his truck and gingerly clipped the seat belt. As he fiddled with the strap of fabric and adjusted it to her size, she had the urge to hug him, to rely on his strength. Her hands remained clasped in her lap, the fingers entwined, squeezing hard.

Henry closed the door and trotted to his side of the vehicle. He jumped in and slammed the door. "Where are we going?"

She told him the address, and he punched it into his GPS.

"Ten minutes," he said.

She nodded and breathed audibly.

He slid a hand across the seat to pull hers into his grasp. She curled her fingers around his warm hand and was instantly grateful he was here with her.

"Why didn't you tell me?" he asked, his voice a near whisper.

"I was going to, but so much has happened lately."

He squeezed her hand, as though acknowledging her dilemma.

"The baby"—she turned to him, still holding his hand—"is yours."

"I know," he said. "Of course, I know."

****

Henry stood with Megan as she went to the desk and told the nurse who she was.

A moment later Dr. Lattimer, a redheaded woman in a loose-fitting white lab coat, greeted Megan and whisked her through a doorway. Henry sat with a thud on an upholstered chair in the waiting room.

The two women seated in the room were in different stages of pregnancy. They cast him appreciative or perhaps sympathetic gazes. He wasn't sure.

Pregnant. Megan was pregnant with his child. His heart was doing funny things in his chest. A kid. A kid of his own. Flesh of his flesh. His gaze wandered to the doorway where just moments ago Megan had disappeared along with her obstetrician.

He didn't know what was wrong, hadn't had the courage to ask her outright, and she hadn't offered any details on the ride over. She had looked pale, worried, and he hated not being able to help her.

Waiting sucked. He wanted to pace the small room, but there was no space, with a round magazine-laden coffee table in the center of the floor and a kiddie area set up on one side. All he could do was stay put and wait. His chest felt as if he'd been bandaged from an injury. Each breath he took was shallow.

Finally, the doctor came through the door and sought him out with her eyes. "Mr. Denhawk, will you come with me, please?"

He hopped up from his seat and stubbed his toe on the table leg. He stifled an expletive and strode across the room.

The doctor escorted him down the hallway to an examining room where Megan sat fully clothed on the crinkly paper-covered table. She held her purse on her lap like a pet.

He went to her. "How are you?" He turned to the doctor. "How is she?"

The doctor's mouth pulled into a sympathetic curve. "Why don't you have a seat?" she said as she motioned to a guest chair.

He hesitated but then sat. The doctor explained that many first-time mothers spotted during their pregnancies. Some women spotted throughout the entire nine months. And with Megan's age, this was considered a high-risk pregnancy, which essentially meant they had to keep a closer watch on her.

The doctor closed her computer and looked directly at Henry. "The important thing is that an ultrasound has shown the fetus is fine. And the cramps could have been gas, or maybe she'd been doing too much." She slid her gaze to Megan. "I know you've got your store opening in a couple of days, but you've said you've got people to help you. Let them. I don't want you on your feet too much, you understand?"

"Yes."

She met Henry's gaze. "Dad, you understand?"

His mind did kind of an explosion. *Dad? Holy shit.*

How he managed to respond with an emphatic nod was beyond him. He locked eyes with Megan, and she looked about as scared shitless as he was.

Chapter Twenty-Two

He kept his mouth shut during the ride back to the shop. He needed to sort out his own thoughts before he formed sentences. At the moment his mind was like a ten-car pileup on the freeway. No rhyme or reason, just a jumble of trouble caused by one twist of fate.

Finally, Megan spoke. "This is a lot to process, I know, Henry."

"It is, but we'll figure it out."

He was sure they would figure it out. People dealt with this kind of situation all the time. But he didn't have answers for Megan now. He was concentrating on breathing.

Back at the store Megan's clerk and Lucy were sorting through a box of baseball cards when he and Megan walked through the door.

They rushed to Megan when she came into the room. They all hugged and uttered words of encouragement while Henry stood by.

"She's got to stay off her feet," he offered.

"Okay, then that's what she'll do."

"With my store opening in two days." Megan took off her jacket and put it on a hook by the front desk. She slung the strap of her purse there as well.

"Come on, you," Lucy said. She pointed to the young clerk. "Henry, this is Mandy. She's a great worker and takes direction well. She and I've got this.

It's your job to convince our friend here that everything's under control."

"Got it," he said. "Hiya, Mandy."

She flashed a broad smile.

Henry had Lucy pegged. Her take-charge attitude in an occasion like this kept her nerves in check. He understood that too well. "Take a seat and order us minions around."

Megan sat on an occasional chair that had a matching ottoman. A sale ticket was affixed to the chairback. "My doctor didn't say I had to sit in one place the whole day. She just said I need to take it easy."

Lucy looked to Henry for verification.

"The doctor doesn't want you on your feet."

Lucy and the girl Megan had hired took direction from Megan, and Henry was confident that the situation was under control. He didn't know his role in this. It was all so new. Was he needed here, or was he in the way?

"What can I do?" he asked.

Megan proffered a rueful smile. "Taking me to the doctor was help enough, Henry. I'm okay. Really."

They had more to say to each other, important things, but that conversation would have to wait.

"Can I get you anything?"

"Henry, I'm good."

Lucy stopped whatever she was doing at the front desk and pointed a finger at him. "You know what we could use? A couple of mums to decorate the front door. You feel like taking a run to the garden store and picking up a couple?"

He looked at Megan. "I can do that."

"Henry, don't worry about mums for now. It's okay."

"Megan, stop," Lucy said. "Let the man be useful. What color do you want him to get?"

"But..."

"What color, Megan?" Lucy insisted.

"If you don't tell me, I'll just decide on my own," Henry said with a hint of a dare.

"Fine. Yellow."

"Yellow it is."

He left the store and was glad for a moment alone to breathe in a lungful of the clean, chilly air. He refused to think, refused to let this latest development settle into his thoughts, knowing the questions that would bombard him.

He drove down Main Street and turned onto Carlyle Road. The garden center was up on the right, and he pulled his truck into the gravel parking lot.

He perused the mum selections. He chose two nicely shaped yellow plants and placed them in a wagon. His gaze fell upon a cluster of purple mums. He selected a nice, healthy, round plant and placed it, too, in his cart. He steered the wagon to the register, and the clerk in a green apron rang up his order.

He stopped and got a pizza and a large container of vegetable soup, along with some sodas, and went back to the Hope Chest to bring the ladies lunch. After they ate, he cleaned up the paper plates and the pizza box.

"Where would you like me to place the mums?"

Megan glanced out the front window. "Um, how about one on each side of the front door?"

She pushed up from her chair, and all eyes riveted to her.

"Oh, come on, you guys," she said. "Stop looking at me like I'm some kind of time bomb. I'm just going out the front door for a minute. Fresh air is good for me, right?"

She followed Henry out while he went to his truck to get the mums. He carried them to the store's front entrance and placed them on either side of the front door.

"How do they look?" he asked.

She smiled at him, and his heart did a kind of somersault. He got the sudden urge to discuss the situation, but with Lucy and Mandy just inside the shop, he kept quiet. Megan was about to host her store's grand opening, and that was what was important at the moment.

Maybe she needed to sort things out in her own head, too. He was still getting his head around the idea that soon another human being would be in his world, a little person that belonged to him, that was part of him. The idea kind of toppled him. He shook thinking about it. And as he slid his gaze over to Megan, he found she was staring at him. Her sweet-tea eyes were filled with question, wonder, and leeriness, all the same things that swam through his veins like hungry fish.

****

The next morning Henry drove into the city to meet with the board regarding his contract. His attorney had posed questions on a couple of points in the verbiage that needed ironing out, but he wasn't concerned. When it came to contract jargon, he trusted Cliff with doing what was best for him.

He texted Megan to see how she was doing this morning, and she responded back that the spotting had stopped and she was feeling well. She promised she would let Mandy do most of the work today while they readied themselves for tomorrow's opening.

He was running late, and Cliff would be having a conniption. He and Cliff had scheduled to meet for breakfast at a place downtown for a pre-meeting meeting, and if his antsy agent got there before him, he'd start texting like a loon.

Henry parked in a garage and strode down the block toward the coffee shop.

Just navigating the busy street, people darting between others on the sidewalk, and the sounds of the city pelting him like rain, he found he could not muster any excitement for the place he'd called home for four years. New York had so much to offer—the nightlife was unmatched—but he did not miss the day-to-day pace of living here in this big metropolis.

His apartment wasn't far from the coffee shop, a nice little one-bedroom on East Sixty-Fourth Street. He did miss his own place. Staying at Sid's apartment had been less than ideal, and if it weren't for the cat, Mookie, he might have commuted to Sycamore River from the city.

After his meeting with the team at the Mets, he'd planned to go check on his apartment. Maybe he'd invite Cliff to join him for a celebration dinner at one of his favorite local haunts.

He stepped into the coffee shop, looked around, saw that he'd beaten Cliff, and found a small table near the back. Cliff breezed in a moment after Henry, and just by the look on his face, Henry knew the man was jazzed for this meeting with the bigwigs of the Mets organization. Cliff lived for the art of the negotiation.

"You ready?" Cliff asked as he shrugged out of his jacket and took a seat across from Henry at the square wooden table. "Did you order?"

"I was waiting for you."

Cliff waved to a server who came by with two laminated menus. The men ordered bagels and coffees and got down to business.

Cliff opened a file he pulled from his briefcase and flipped to a page. "Okay, let's get it straight about the renewal policy. As the contract stands—"

"Megan's pregnant."

Cliff stopped midsentence and just stared at him. "Who the hell is Megan?"

"You know—Megan. The girl you talked with at the luncheon after Sid's funeral. Longish chestnut-colored hair, great big brown eyes. My stepfather's tenant."

"The one from the cemetery?"

"Yes. Her."

"Are you shitting me, Hank?" Cliff closed the file with a flourish. "I told you to be nice to a girl like that, not bed her down, for God's sake. Jesus, you're fast. When did you find this out? Why didn't you call me?"

"First off, calm down. Second, it turns out I knew the lady prior to my going back to Sycamore River. And I just found out yesterday."

"And you're sure this is your problem?"

He didn't like Cliff's reference to Megan's pregnancy as a "problem." It didn't sit well with him.

"Cliff, I'll work this out, okay? Don't get your panties in a bunch."

Cliff shook his head. "You sure about that?"

"Positive."

"Okay, Casanova, you handle it." He swore under his breath.

The server delivered their coffees and bagels, and the two men spent a few short minutes involved in their breakfasts. His head swarmed with thoughts, but he kept quiet. Henry didn't even want to look over to Cliff for fear of getting him going again.

"Let's be real about this, Hank. This situation isn't going away. Let me handle it for you like I've done all the other times."

"What other times?" As far as he knew, there were no other pregnancies on his horizon.

"The chick from LA who said you promised to marry her, the actress who said you were supposed to rent her a place of her own when you broke up, the one here in town who tried to say you were her baby's daddy and then for the handsome sum of five Gs admitted you two had never even done the deed. Remember those fun times, Henry? Yeah, I was the one that made them go away. I swear, if this woman decides to cause you trouble, this beautiful deal we've wrangled for you could go up in smoke. You do realize that, don't you?"

"That's not going to happen. This is different."

Cliff blew out a long breath. "It always is."

Chapter Twenty-Three

Around five o'clock they closed shop. Megan promised Mandy that she would go home and rest for tomorrow's big day. Lucy, who'd stopped in to check on her, also made her confirm she would be home for dinner. She heated water for tea on the burner in the back room using a small saucepan as a makeshift kettle, deciding she didn't want to leave just yet.

The store was ready. Looking around at everything, she was happy. The Hope Chest would open for business tomorrow. How long had the idea of a thrift shop been just a wish in her heart? Now here it was, a place for people to come and find treasures that would make their lives just a little better, a bit happier. She shook her head. She'd always been a bit of a romantic, but lately her hormones were kicking her emotions into overdrive.

She shut off the burner and poured the hot water into her mug. Letting the teabag steep, she heard a noise in the front of the store. She left the back room to find a man, carrying a black leather briefcase, had come in through the front door. She recognized him as Henry's agent. Cliff.

"Hello. Cliff, isn't it?" Something inside told her this wasn't a social call. His dark eyes riveted to hers and held her gaze, making her uncomfortable. She looked away and tried to dismiss the uneasiness. But today was the big meeting with the people from the Mets. Had something gone wrong? A tightness clenched at her chest. Had Gemma done what she'd threatened? Had she told her secret to Henry? She had to shut her brain off before she made herself sick.

"Can I help you?"

He made a point of looking around as he came deeper into the space. "Boy, this place is looking sharp. Very sharp."

"Thank you." *See? There's no problem.* "We are opening tomorrow for the first time."

"Much success."

"Are you looking for Henry? Because he's not here. I thought you were in the city with him."

"I was. When our meeting ended, he went over to check on his apartment, and I came back to Sycamore River to have a chat with you."

"With me? I don't understand."

"Why don't you have a seat, Megan?" He sat in a kitchen chair that was part of a four-part set. He pulled one out for her.

"What's this about?" She reluctantly sat in the chair.

"Oh, I think you know."

Her face flushed. Was it the pregnancy? Was it her past? Both? Ire climbed up her spine. "What exactly do you have to say?"

"As I'm sure you know, Megan, Henry Denhawk is a very busy guy, a man who is going to be part of major league baseball again after a long hiatus. This is something he and I have worked toward for a long time. And this situation you've found yourself in shouldn't stand in his way. It won't stand in his way."

Her heart raced in her chest. Henry had told him about the baby. "I don't expect Henry to change his plans, if that's what you're saying."

"What do you expect from him, Megan?"

"Shouldn't I be having this conversation with Henry and not you?"

"I do all Henry's negotiations. That's my job. And I'm here today to make you an offer. Having a baby, I'm sure, is not easy, especially when you're a single mother. Henry is sympathetic to that point, please understand. But he's not going to have much time to involve himself in the day-to-day with you and your child. You should have realized that before you, shall we say, went down that road. That said, Henry's prepared to assist in this. As long as you'll submit to a paternity test, Henry would be willing to give you a monthly payment for your trouble and for the baby's needs. We'll make it all nice and tidy with our attorney's help. How does that sound?"

"Does Henry know you're here making this offer to me?"

"Whose money do you think I'm offering you? Certainly not mine, Megan."

"Then you can tell Mr. Denhawk that I won't be needing his help or his money. I will not take a paternity test, and asking me for one is an insult considering that he's well aware that there's been no one else. And, sir, I'd like you to leave. I need to close up the store."

Cliff stood and gave her a smarmy smile. "I know about that woman in Chicago. Gemma Lang, your so-called aunt. She's not a very nice person, I'm thinking. Doesn't have too many nice things to say about you,

Megan. Is it true you're a petty thief?"

"Get out."

"You'll be hearing from Henry's attorney, in case you rethink the matter and decide to take Henry's generous offer."

She didn't bother to respond and just stared at him until he walked through the store and left. Bitter tears clouded her eyes. What happened to the man who carried her out of the store and held her hand on the way to her doctor's office, the man who did odds and ends around the shop so that she wouldn't have to? Was that all for show? Was that all fake? Or had he simply had a chance to think it over and realize that being part of her and their baby's life was not what he wanted? She wiped away the tears. She wouldn't let Henry Denhawk make her feel bad. This was her life and her baby. He could go right straight to hell.

Chapter Twenty-Four

Henry sat in his apartment and took it all in. It was a nice place, tasteful, uncomplicatedly minimalistic. He thought of Megan's store and the furnishings she was peddling. None of her items would fit in this apartment.

He went room to room and looked at the apartment as though he were a guest who had never seen it. The space reminded him of a suite in a high-end hotel. Clean, neat, and efficient—and if he were honest, impersonal.

He remembered the fridge still had some beer in it, and he pulled a bottle into his hands and twisted off the cap. He took a long pull.

The contract with the Mets had been ironed out. As soon as they managed to make the changes, a few deletions and additions, and his attorney gave him the go-ahead, he'd sign and be an official part of the organization again. He took another sip of his beverage.

He never really thought he'd be involved in major league baseball again. Those days had been packed away like an old uniform or a high school yearbook. But now here was his chance to make things right again, make his life count again, undo his sins of the past. As the new guy on the broadcasting team, he would begin his career with the away-game schedule. Eighty-one games on the road. That was a lot. He took another long pull of his beer.

He thought of the money. They were offering him less than the others were making—he knew that without even knowing the figures—but he also knew what a coup this opportunity was.

He finished the beer, rinsed the bottle, and put the empty into the recycle bin. He'd be home in New York sooner than he thought. Once the contract was modified and signed by all parties, he'd be expected to report to work, learn the ropes. Where was he going to find the time to deal with Sid's estate? What about Megan? Where did she fit into all of this? If he could find a way to work out his schedule, how would that play out with Megan? Where did his heart belong among all these moving parts? Was it with Megan? Would she even want him if he put his heart on the line?

The one thing he did know was that he and Megan needed to have an important conversation. And soon.

****

On his way back to Sycamore River, Henry stopped off at Gate of Heaven Cemetery. The purple mum he'd purchased the other day was still in the back of his truck, and he wanted to replace the dried-out plant with this new one. He didn't have any tools for such things at his apartment, so he'd stopped off at a hardware store and bought himself a cheap trowel and a jug of water.

The jug of water in one hand, the trowel jammed into his jacket pocket, and the mum tucked in the crook of his other arm, he made his way to his mother's grave. He placed the items on the ground.

Sid's grave was still dirt. The flowers from the funeral home that had been strewn over the area had been removed by the grounds crew, and grass seeds had been planted in the patch of earth. He thought of how the old man had left him his estate, still confused about how and why that happened.

He thought of the day here with Megan and how she'd had a conversation with her deceased husband. She'd told him recently that she believed messages came not in words but in feelings, as long as you had faith.

He fixed his gaze on Sid's stone and cleared his throat.

"Sid, um, I had hoped to get the chance to say goodbye to you at the hospital, but you checked out before I could. I'm still surprised, shocked actually, that you left me your estate. I know what you've thought about me. At least I thought I did."

He looked around to make sure no one was nearby. He suddenly felt a little crazy. His gaze fell to Sid's son's grave beside his. Andrew's headstone had a carved heart in the upper left corner above the engraving of his name, birthdate, and day of death. Henry zeroed in on words etched into the stone.

Our Champion, A short life well lived

How had Henry never noticed that before? Had he ever really looked at Andrew's headstone? He was ashamed. Andrew had been the light of Sid's life, and true to the epitaph, his life had been cut too short, and he had lived well. Andrew had been a good kid, a boy who worked his ass off in school, had been an admirable teammate on his school's baseball team. Far from being a star, he'd hung in even when his main position was bench. Andrew had been a champion.

"Rest in peace, Andrew," he said before he even realized the words had slipped from his lips.

He glanced again at Sid's grave. He thought about Sid's definition of a champion. Would he ever meet that criterion? Could he be his best self no matter the circumstance? He tipped an imaginary hat. "I'm working on it, Sid."

It was getting late, he'd be losing daylight, and he still had to switch the mums. He stepped over to his mother's grave and, bending down, tugged the dying purple mum from where it had been planted in the area in front of her stone.

"Well, Mom—" He paused to look up at her name engraved in the granite. "—I don't know if you're up there listening or anything, but in case you are, I want you to know that I'm going to be a father. Yup. Me. I wish this baby could have known you."

A lump formed in his throat. He tugged on the dying plant some more, using the trowel to chop into the hard earth and to loosen the roots that clung to the soil.

"My, um, my baby's mother is the one who told me that it was a good thing to talk to you like this. You'd like her, Mom. She's something special. The thing is, I don't know what our future is because I got this new job with the Mets. Yeah, how about that, right? I'm going to commentate at the games. It's exciting, but the job's going to take me away from home a lot. A real lot. I mean, I'm going to have a child. That's big. I don't know. I wish I knew the answer to all this."

He finally loosened the mum's roots enough for the plant to pull free into his grasp. He took the brown-bloomed lump and brought it to the metal trash can at the end of the aisle. As he was about to toss the bundle, he spotted something shiny. He pushed aside the dry shoots, and amid the messy tangle he knew exactly what he was looking at.

A small brass key.

Chapter Twenty-Five

On his way home to feed Mookie and give him his medicine, Henry tried to call Megan. He couldn't believe he'd actually found the key to the hope chest. He thought of his conversation with her and her belief in messages from loved ones who had passed. Was the key some kind of message?

More likely that key had fallen from Megan's pocket on the day Cliff's damn dog chased her around the headstones. The key had probably fallen into the dirt surrounding the plant, and there it sat.

Yet he'd been the one to find it on the first and only time he'd told his mother that he wished she were there to give him advice. He uttered a soft incredulous laugh. Could it be?

His head was filled with so many thoughts, different scenarios on how to make his new situations work. Being out of the city and back in his hometown gave him a feeling of coming home even though, technically, the apartment he'd just come from was his home.

Megan didn't answer his call or his text. She was busy, he knew, with the store's opening slotted for tomorrow. He'd see her tomorrow, for sure, but he needed to know she was feeling okay before he went to bed.

Two more calls and two more nonanswers and he

got into his truck and drove over to Lucy's house. He needed to see how she was for himself.

****

Megan was never more disappointed in one human being than she was in Henry Denhawk. She sat at her laptop on the kitchen table and stared at his damn face in a picture on some media gossip site. The photo was from an earlier time. He was wearing a Mets jersey and was smiling into the camera as if he owned the whole damned world. The caption announced that he was the Mets' new color commentator for the upcoming major league season.

She closed the laptop and made herself a cup of tea.

Lucy came into the room and slipped an arm around Megan's shoulders. "Want me to kill him?"

"Yes, please."

"Go sit, Megs. I'll make us both teas."

She didn't argue but sat back at the table. She put her sock-covered feet on the chair across from her. She was tired, dog tired, weary. Tomorrow was a big day, the day she had anticipated for so long. And Henry Denhawk had spoiled that for her, too.

She hadn't thought that the baby she was carrying would make them an instant family, but she hadn't expected for his goon to come and give her his sleazy offer to basically keep her mouth shut. The whole thing made her sick.

The doorbell rang, and she and Lucy exchanged a look. Henry had called her a few times, and she hadn't taken the calls. She had nothing to say to the man. He'd texted to see how she was feeling, but she'd decided he'd lost his right to know. She hoped that new job of his took him to Timbuktu.

Lucy walked out of the kitchen and went to the front door. Megan heard the murmuring between her friend and the voice she knew was Henry's. Her heart turned to a block of ice in her chest. The coldness ached.

Lucy came into the room, and with a shrug she said, "He wouldn't go away. I told him he's got five minutes."

Henry came into the kitchen with an odd look on his face. He seemed confused, a look that would fool just about anyone into thinking that he was sincere in his concern for her. She was not fooled. Not this time.

"I'll be in the living room if you need me, Megs," Lucy said. She flashed Henry a look. "Upset her, and you deal with me."

After she left the room, Henry went right to Megan. "What's going on? Are you okay? Lucy's acting weird. Why haven't you answered any of my calls or texts?"

"Henry, what is there left to say?" She heard the weariness in her tone. "You shouldn't have come here."

"I'm so confused. Are you angry with me?"

She laughed a mirthless sound. "No. I'd have to actually care to be mad at you. And I don't."

"Wait, what? Can you please talk to me?"

"There's really nothing to say, Henry. Look, I'll make this easy on you, okay? This is my baby. Mine. You don't need to worry about me or it, and you can just go and live your big new life. Just please leave me alone, and I'll do the same."

"Megan—"

"My store is opening tomorrow. I'm tired, and I

just want you to leave."

"But I—"

"You heard her, man. She'd like you to leave." Lucy stood in the doorway to the kitchen with her arms folded over her chest. "You two can talk another time when Megan feels like it. Until then, good night."

He hesitated and tried to get her to talk, but she was not interested. He attempted to at least meet her gaze, but she turned her head.

Finally, he let Lucy escort him to the door. Megan could hear the sound of his truck as it slowly went down the road and drove away from her.

Chapter Twenty-Six

Henry hadn't slept much. He kept going over Megan's words, the look on her face. She had cut him out of her life with one swift slice.

Cliff called him with the news that the Mets organization had come up with the final and complete version of the contract and wanted him to review it with his attorney. They emailed the contract to Cliff, and he sounded excited.

"Hank, this is a thing of beauty." Cliff's voice was loud, animated. "All it needs is your signature. But, of course, we let the attorney give you the go-ahead."

He agreed with Cliff that the document needed to go to his attorney, and then, in the beginning of the week, the Mets people were expecting this to be a done deal.

His mind wouldn't go there, not today. All he had in his head was Megan and her one-eighty. She still didn't answer his calls or his texts. She was done with him. But he had rights, didn't he? This was his baby, too. Whether or not she wanted to be in his company didn't cancel out the fact that he had a right to be in his child's life. Would he need an attorney for that, too? His head ached.

"Hank, come on, bro, what's with you today? Why aren't you jumping for joy with this? We got just what we wanted."

"I know, Cliff. I appreciate it all, believe me. It's just that I've got some other things on my mind, that's all." He reached into his pocket and withdrew the brass key he'd found at the cemetery. He rubbed the pad of his thumb over the burnished metal.

Cliff chuckled. "Fear not. I've fixed that, too, my friend."

He snapped to attention. "What'd you say?"

"Just like any other time, I worked my magic. Problem solved."

"What problem?"

"You know. The girl with the bun in the oven."

"Megan? You talked to Megan?"

"Of course, I did. You think I was going to let some woman come along and suppress you with her guilt trip? I have to tell you she didn't give me a hard time either. Easiest kiss-off yet."

"What did you do, Cliff?" His voice boomed into his cell phone. "What the fuck did you do?"

Cliff reiterated his conversation with Megan, and while his agent droned on, Henry was glad he couldn't reach through the phone and wring the stupid man's scrawny neck.

"Oh, and guess what else? I did some digging and found out she never even graduated high school. Quit in her senior year, and you know why? She was busy stealing from a bodega. Wound up in juvenile hall, then took off. Good riddance to that one. The last thing you'd need is to get hooked up with her and have the media find out about her antics of the past. Can you imagine?"

"Who gave you the right to do any of that? You just took that upon yourself to dig into her life and then mess with her and me?"

"Did you hear me, man? She was a juvenile delinquent, for God's sake."

"How dare you, Cliff? How fucking dare you?"

"What are you talking about? I'm the fixer. You mess up—which you've done more times than I can recall, mind you—and I fix it. That's our partnership."

"Not anymore it's not. I told you to stay out of this. I'm done. Done with you."

Cliff laughed. "You're not serious. What? Do you have feelings for this woman? Come on, Hank, you're not thinking clearly. Hey, okay, look, you want to see the kid sometimes, so I'm sure I can arrange—"

"No," he bellowed. "Stop. Stay out of it. I swear to God, Cliff. Stop."

He disconnected the call and sat there in Sid's living room, the key in the palm of his hand. He'd known Megan's growing up had been lousy, and the fact that she'd quit school and had somehow gotten into trouble stealing had to have been need driven. He knew her, and she was the most honorable person he'd ever met. Like a reel of vintage footage, he thought back to all his mistakes, all the things he'd done wrong over the years. Not just baseball, but that, too. Mostly, though, he thought about the disconnect he'd lived with his own life. He'd spent so much time either screwing up his career or wishing he still had it, feeling like he was a nobody because what used to be was done.

Again, he thought of Andrew's epitaph. Sid's son had had a short life but had lived it well. What had he done? His heart hammered in his chest. He gripped the object in his hand. Suddenly he was completely clear on what to do, what he wanted to do more than anything he'd ever wanted in his whole life.

    He pushed up from the couch. He had so much to do.

Chapter Twenty-Seven

The grand opening of the Hope Chest had been a success. Megan dutifully spent a lot of her time sitting on a chair in her witch's hat, handing out candy and business cards to adults and candy bars to the kids who came into her store.

So many kind, complimentary people came in to browse. Each purchase was like matching someone with something that would make their life just a little better.

Carolyn Montgomery came by to offer congratulations. Megan was touched by the gesture. She watched as Carolyn perused the shelves and was practically knocked speechless when she walked over to Megan with the cut-glass gravy boat in her hands.

"This is only ten dollars?"

"Yes," Megan said. "It's lovely, isn't it?"

"It's just so pretty." She tilted her head. "I'd like to buy it."

"Great. Mandy's at the register. She can ring you up."

"This is a really nice store, Megan. You must be proud."

"Thanks, Carolyn. How's your son?"

"He's doing better. Did you know Henry has contacted him twice and has even offered to help him get his arm in shape when he's able to practice?"

Megan's heart thundered. "He did?"

She nodded. "We're so grateful for his help. Well, thank you again for this." She lifted the gravy boat in her hands. "And best of luck with the shop."

The store was busy nonstop, and the time flew by. Megan couldn't believe how many familiar faces had come to the opening.

Sycamore River had a lot of affluence in it these days with the effects of the gentrification. But the backbone to this town was the townspeople. They were the ones who lived in and loved this corner of the world back when it was a small village with one pharmacy, one bakery, and a greengrocer. The big brick and mortars and subdivisions of today might have changed the landscape a bit, but they didn't change the heart of this town. Her town.

Those people were her customer base. The Hope Chest existed for them, and her eyes misted at the thought that her dream had come to fruition.

In truth, though, she'd done nothing but shed tears for two days. Ever since that awful man, Henry's goon, had treated her like a blemish on the magical, idyllic life of the Hawk. How dare he, but mostly, how dare Henry.

When five o'clock came, the Hope Chest's official first day was complete. She and Mandy hugged each other.

"We did it." Mandy beamed. "How do you feel?"

"Well, isn't this a fine-looking establishment?" a voice rang out from the entrance.

Heart stalled in her chest, Megan turned to the voice, although she already knew who it was. Aunt Gemma.

Gemma and a man came in closer, each of them wearing a snarky look.

"Congratulations, baby girl," Gemma said. "Successful first day, was it?"

"What are you doing here? How did you get here?"

"I came to see you, and my friend Paulie here drove us. Took all night." Gemma fingered the display of tablecloths. "I had a bunch of these. Who knew you could get money for them nowadays?"

Mandy leaned close to Megan. "Is everything okay?"

Megan nodded. "I've got this. You can head out."

Mandy shook her head. "I'm sticking around."

"Where's that famous boyfriend of yours?" Gemma snickered. "We'd like to meet him."

"He's not my boyfriend. So you can turn right around and head back to Chicago. I've got nothing more to say to you."

"Oh, you don't, huh? I'm guessing that means you haven't changed your mind about giving me a raise?"

Megan's heart hammered in her chest. She had spent the day greeting people, interacting with her neighbors, and just enjoying the warmth of belonging. She'd be damned if she'd let this selfish woman steal that from her. Not anymore.

She went to the cash register and pushed the button for the drawer to pop open. She withdrew some bills, then counted out what she felt was enough.

She went over to Gemma and handed her the stack of bills. "This should be enough for you and your friend to buy gasoline and some food for your trip home. Now I'd like you to leave."

Gemma laughed, and so did her friend, whom

Megan suspected had no idea what he was laughing at. "You can't mean that, baby doll. I've got the power to ruin you."

"No, Gemma. You do not. Here's the thing. I let you push me around all this time, gave you money so you'd leave me alone. That was my mistake. I should have told you to go to hell back then. But I guess better late than never. We're done, Gemma. There will be no more money from me."

"You're a fool." Gemma's voice was filled with rage. "I'll blab all there is to blab about you. How would your famous boyfriend like to know his precious Megan is a thief? You don't care how that will tarnish his reputation?"

"I told you. He is not my boyfriend. Don't make me call the police, Gemma."

"Come on," Paulie said as he took Gemma's arm. "Take the money she's offered, and let's go."

She yanked her arm free of him. "I gave you a life," she shouted. "You ungrateful, illiterate girl."

Megan zeroed in on Paulie's gaze. "You probably don't want any trouble. Convince her it's time to go."

"Come on, Gem." He put his arm around her. "Who needs her, right? Let's go."

Gemma met her gaze. "You'll be sorry." She yanked the bills from Megan's still-extended hand.

"Goodbye, Gemma. For once and for all."

The couple left, and Megan dashed to the front door and locked it. She turned the Open sign over to display Closed to the outside. She put her forehead on the doorjamb and pulled air into her lungs.

Whatever repercussions Gemma might dish out would not take away from the relief of feeling free for the first time in so many years.

Mandy came up and touched her shoulder. "Oh my God, Megan. Who was that?"

She turned to her young employee. "Someone I used to know."

"She's awful."

Megan gave her a rueful smile. Yeah. Gemma Lang was pretty damn awful. But she was gone, and Megan had her life back. Nothing would take that away from her.

"You must be tired," Mandy said.

"I am. But it's kind of a good, satisfying tired, if you know what I mean."

"How about we count the cash drawer, and then I'll lock up," Mandy said.

"Thank you, Mandy."

After performing the task, Megan grabbed her jacket and purse. "Thank you for all your help today, Mandy."

"You are more than welcome."

"Please take the leftover candy with you. Share it with your roommate."

The girl grinned. "That's a deal."

****

That night Megan tried watching a show on TV, but her mind was elsewhere. She had cut Gemma loose regardless of her threats. Both relief and apprehension tingled on her skin. She cradled her belly and silently spoke to her child, telling the baby they would be okay.

Her cell phone sounded, and her first instinct was that it was Henry calling. She saw it was Mandy, and her heart fell despite herself. She connected the call.

"Megan, how are you feeling?"

"Fine, good. Thanks so much for all your help today."

"Can you come back to the store for a few?"

"Now?" She consulted her fitness tracker. It was pushing eight o'clock. What was she still doing there?

"Yes," Mandy said. "Just for a little while. I want to show you something."

"What is it? Does this have anything to do with my visitors?"

"No, no, nothing like that."

"Is everything okay?"

"Yes, of course. It's just that, well, you have to see something yourself. I can't explain it."

"I'll be there in a few."

She ended the call and got ready. After one day as an official store owner, she was surprised at just how deep her connection was to the shop. Mandy sounded odd. Megan couldn't put her finger on it.

She drove over to the store and parked in front. A low light was on inside, the beam familiar. It came from the glass lamp on a piecrust table near the front of the store.

She unlocked the door and went inside. Mandy was nowhere to be found, but standing up in the front of the store was Henry Denhawk.

"What are you doing here? Where's Mandy?"

"I begged her to let me in and then to call you. Don't be mad at her. I was relentless."

"This is ridiculous. You had no business doing that to her. Unbelievable."

"I needed a chance for you to hear me out, and this is the only thing I could think of."

She folded her arms, mostly to keep herself from

shivering. Just seeing him there in his jeans and that dark blue shirt did something to her insides. She hated him or wanted to with all her heart.

"Well, you've got me here. Say what you want to say."

"Mandy told me that the shop was a hit today."

"It was."

"Congratulations."

"Thank you, but this isn't why we're here, is it?"

"No." He took a step in her direction, a tentative step, as though he were afraid she'd run away.

She stood her ground.

He put his head down, then looked back up at her. "I know what Cliff did to you."

"I'm sure you do."

"I just found out today. I didn't know what he had done, and I absolutely did not tell him to say or do anything. That was all him. And I've fired him for it."

Her insides folded in on themselves. "What?"

"What he said to you, Megan, makes me sick." He came closer. "I'd never do that to you. You have to believe me. I'll admit that when I first learned you were pregnant, I was kind of stunned maybe, but never, not once did I think I wanted to escape the reality of this. Not ever."

"And I'm sure he told you about my past, how I quit high school and was arrested for stealing."

"He did. But I know you, and I know you had to have your reasons for whatever you did. Besides, who knows better than I that what we once did doesn't have to be who we become?"

Unbidden tears came to her eyes with a stinging sensation. She swallowed, could not speak.

Finally, she found her voice. "I had to leave school and home to get away from the situation with my aunt. I got a job. The owner got handsy and fired me when I wouldn't comply. So I took what he owed me out of his register. He pressed charges on me."

He took a step closer. "Megan." His eyes shone with wetness. "I'm sorry."

"I got another job and got my GED all on my own." Tears slid down her face.

"Megan, listen to me." He was very near her now, so near she could smell his piney-scented cologne. "I'm sure you know that the Mets and I came to satisfactory terms with their offer."

She nodded.

"I went to the cemetery after I met with them. I had a conversation while I was there." His mouth slid into a crooked, sheepish smile, and her heart lurched. "A couple of conversations, actually."

"Did you?"

"I told Sid that I didn't know why on earth he'd leave me everything he had, but I promised him that I would be more of a man he'd have been proud of."

She couldn't help it. The tears kept pouring down her cheeks.

"Then I had a few words with my mother. She had these purple mums there by her headstone, ones Sid had planted before he got sick. And when I was there for the funeral, I noticed that the plant was looking pretty sickly. So when I went to the garden store, I got her a replacement plant. Got a trowel to dig up the old one and everything."

She continued to listen, unable to form words. She knew how he had felt about those who talked to their dead loved ones. He'd changed. She didn't know what to make of it, but her heart had started to beat with something fragile but true, something like hope.

"While I was doing my gardening work, I found something I thought you'd like to have."

He pulled a small box from his pocket. It looked like a ring box, but she knew it couldn't be a ring. Where would he get a ring at a cemetery? What was he even talking about?

He extended it to her. "Open it."

She took the box and met his gaze. "What is this?"

He shrugged, his smile broadening.

She opened the box, and there on the black velvet was the key to her hope chest. "The key." She took it into her hand. "Where on earth did you find this?"

"It was tangled in a clump of dried roots inside the mum I removed from my mother's grave. It was by sheer luck that I spotted it."

She stared at it, then met his gaze. Sheer luck? "Thank you," she managed.

"Aren't you going to see if it works?"

"What?"

He motioned his head toward the piece of furniture up by the front window.

"Oh, right, yes," she said, feeling flustered. She went to the chest, slipped the key into the lock, and turned it. The cabinet lid opened.

She peered inside. The cabinet was no longer empty. She looked to Henry and back to the chest. She pulled out a silver picture frame, then another, then another. No pictures, just empty frames.

"Megan Harris." Henry came up to her. "Will you make memories with me, share moments we can photograph and put in those frames? There's not much of a chance we'll have a grand piano in our house to display them, but I'm sure we can put them on the mantel of the small Craftsman on River Road. I reached out to Lucy, and she said it's still available. I told her not to sell it to anyone until she hears from us. Let's buy it, Megan."

"What? You contacted Lucy?"

"Come with me, Megan, and help me make that house our home, our baby's home. Help me make Sycamore River be my home again. I've contacted Coach Lou and told him I'd like to help him start up the baseball clinic he's been wanting to establish. We're going to be partners. We have our first recruit, too. Joshua Montgomery can't wait to sign on."

"But—but what about being a baseball broadcaster?"

"I had to turn them down."

"You turned them down?"

A broad smile broke across his lips. "I've had a change of dreams."

"You're serious."

He stepped closer still. He was just a breath away. "I have a feeling my family is going to keep me too busy to work out of town. Will it, love? Will you and our baby have me?"

She threw her arms around him. "Henry," she managed to croak. "Henry."

He kissed her then, trailed kisses over her cheeks as though to banish her tears.

"Megan," he said as he met her gaze. "I love you, and I already love the life we're going to make together. A life well lived."

A word about the author…

Born to a feisty Italian mother and a gentle blue-eyed Irishman, multi-award-winning author M. Kate Quinn draws on her quirky sense of humor, hopelessly romantic nature, highly developed sense of family and friendship, and her love for a good story while writing her novels.

She has been a Golden Quill Awards finalist, a Golden Leaf Awards winner and finalist, and a Heart of Excellence Readers' Choice Award winner. Her latest project, The Sycamore River Series, is a trilogy of romances set in a quaint New Jersey town. The first installment, *Saying Yes to the Mess*, was released in August 2018. *Mr. Maybe* was released in August 2019. *The Hope Chest* is the third and final book in the series.

M. Kate Quinn, a lifelong native of New Jersey, and her husband make their home in Central Jersey, where they enjoy big, raucous gatherings with their large family and three amazing grandchildren.

Thank you for purchasing
this publication of The Wild Rose Press, Inc.

For questions or more information
contact us at
info@thewildrosepress.com.

The Wild Rose Press, Inc.
www.thewildrosepress.com